SHATTERED ICE

Fury #3

MONTY JAY

Copyright

"There are darknesses in life and there are lights, and you are one of the lights, the light of all lights."

Bram Stoker, Dracula

To the girls who are children of the universe. You are the sun, the moon, the stars. You are galaxies. Do not settle for someone who doesn't bathe in your cosmic wonder.

Playlist

Complicated-Avril Lavigne
I'm With You-Avril Lavigne
My Happy Ending-Avril Lavigne
Things I'll Never Say-Avril Lavigne
Galway Girl-Ed Sheeran
Roman Holiday-Halsey
The Middle-Jimmy Eat World
Ocean Avenue-Yellowcard
Cold-Crossfade
Stacy's Mom-Fountains of Wayne
In My Veins-Andrew Belle
Wrong Side of Heaven-Five Finger Death Punch
Battle Born-Five Finger Death Punch
Remember Everything-Five Finger Death Punch
Move Along-All American Rejects
Throne-Bring Me the Horizon
I'll be Good-Jaymes Young
Get You-Daniel Caesar
Scars-Papa Roach
Never too Late-Three Days Grace

All I Wanted-Paramore
Check Yes, Juliet-We the Kings
Let Me Sign-Robert Pattinson
From Eden-Hozier
Cherry Wine-Hozier
Sweet Thing-Hozier
Arsonist's Lullabye-Hozier
Angel of Small Death and The Codeine Scene-Hozier
Outnumbered-Dermot Kennedy
Power Over Me-Dermot Kennedy
Old Money-Lana Del Rey
My Love-Sia
Mansion-NF
Fallen Angel-Three Days Grace
River Of Tears-Alessia Cara
Don't Forget About Me-Cloves

Prologue

KAI

I'd never quite understood the point of eulogies. I mean be realistic, who the hell cares?

I had already made my way to the podium standing in front of a room full of people, dressed in a pair of black slacks and matching button-down. A tie didn't seem fully necessary for the occasion. Although I'm sure some would beg to differ.

I lean into the microphone knowing very well the people awaiting my speech are sitting on the edge of their seat to hear what I have to say about the loss of this loved one.

I clear my throat, wetting my lips that are already moist, just pulling my audience in closer like a spider to their succulent web. The front row was mostly women my mother's age, eyeing me up and down like I wasn't sixteen.

In their line of work age was just a number anyway. It didn't matter how low or how high as long as a profit was on the other side. Hook, line, and sinker, if I wanted them, I could have them.

Wickedly twisted, isn't it? I'm not sure what's worse, the fact I am so absurdly confident in my conclusion, or that it's true.

Upside down, sideways, in a car, two at a time, right fucking here in front of my dead mother I could have them, legs spread, back shoved into the ground. I think they fed off the fact that I knew they wanted me, but I didn't want them.

"Death is not the greatest loss in life. The greatest loss is what dies inside us while we live."

The words written by Norman Cousins glide effortlessly off my tongue. They may as well be my own.

I nod my head, pushing my palm through my growing hair. It's about shoulder length, so it might be time to cut it. But I probably won't.

Back to eulogies, why must I spend time writing out something for someone I should have told things to when they were alive? What was the point now?

The person I'm talking about is dead.

Cold as ice, or possibly room temperature because of the embalming fluid, but all together dead. Unless you believed in the afterlife. Which I, sadly, did not. She can't hear anything I'm saying about her, not like she would care if she could.

My mother never was the motherly type.

The entire point of this for lack of a better word, morbid speech, is attention. People thrive off attention from these things. Death and freak accidents. Everyone wants to be the best friend of a lost loved one so people watch them cry and say,

"Oh that poor soul, they must be devastated."

That's what eulogies are. Just a public deceleration of your relationship with the dead so people know who to feel sorry for. But here is the thing,

I was never the son type.

I also didn't need anyone feeling sorry for me. What did sorry ever do for me? Not a fucking goddamn thing.

I move away from my spot, headed down the aisle to exit the church. The funeral wasn't over but my part in it sure as fuck was. My speech took all of three seconds. I did my part, now I could leave.

The minuscule group of people watch me in shock, evading my own mother's funeral. How cruel. What kind of son am I? Not even a single tear for the women who gave birth to me.

There are things much worse than death, I assure you.

Not to mention nearly every single person who is in attendance is either drunk or twenty seconds away from their next high. I'm not judging by their outfits or rotten teeth either, I know this for an absolute fact.

I grew up around these women and the men who are in charge of their bodies. I lived among prostitutes and pimps in the city of St. Petersburg. The hysterical thing about the entire situation is a church is what hides the money.

Holy ground turned sinister because of money. Drugs, sex, guns, didn't matter as long as the check was signed to Saint Mary's Church of Mercy. It was a *don't look, don't ask questions* kind of church.

I still found it funny watching from the rafters as the people piled inside for mass or to confess their sins. I'd sit up there with stale bread, a tattered book, wearing dirty clothes. They all walked in with fancy dresses, tailored suits, throwing their money onto the gold plate. They were worshiping a place that housed young girls being pimped, a house that kept people like me a secret, hidden in the shadows. The church was the face of hell.

I was a product of pimps and preachers.

I loved cackling at the priest who would lecture for hours about sins, how the world we lived in was a dirty place and how the Lord would cleanse it.

Maybe he was saying that to clear his own dirty conscience. Maybe if he said it enough in mass the Lord would cleanse his soul. I highly doubt it though.

Let's just say in his free time he wasn't planning his next bible lesson while he was reading the tattoo on Jasmine's lower back because she was bent over his office desk while he tried to keep it up.

The joys of hypocrisy. Gotta love it.

I'm not knocking religion. If you want to worship a goat, I don't give a shit. I don't condone using something meant to be pure like religion as a mask or a gateway to do bad things. You don't need religion to have morals and just because you are religious doesn't mean your morals are right.

To those in charge of these working girls, they were helping them. Doing the Lord's will by assisting them out of poverty. The church gave them clothing, food, housing, warmth. All in exchange for them to spread their legs. To them it was an easy trade.

My father, not sure of his name, don't think I care either, was a random John. I'm not particularly sure why my mother went through with the pregnancy. Lots of women in that line of work get abortions. It's more common than giving birth, but apparently my mother was adamant on having me.

I push the doors open to be met with the frigid cold wind that accompanies the wet snow pouring down from the sky. My breath becomes visible as I release a breath from deep inside my lungs.

"Where do you think you are going, мой мальчик?"

My boy.

I wasn't anyone's goddamn boy. I never had been. I'd always just been a bastard born in a brothel.

My shoulders tense, my jaw clenches tightly. The smell of her fruity cigar wafts through the air and I find it more difficult to hate her. There was something about menthol scents that soothed me. The smoke smelled like peppermint.

This woman who shared my eyes. I wanted to hate her, but I couldn't. Which was odd considering it was odder for me to love someone. However, it was hard to hate someone who radiated so much love.

"Not with you, Nina," I grunt, looking at the falling snowflakes and slushy covered streets with a bored expression.

My signature emotionless face. The boy without a smile they called me in school. Teachers, students, principals.

"Malakai, you can't stay angry with me." She exclaims, "I wasn't even aware you existed until I heard the news about your mother! We weren't exactly on great terms."

I would give her that one. I believed her when she had told me she wasn't aware of my existence. My mother didn't need the police banging on the front door yanking me out of there and arresting everyone for prostitution.

I'm surprised she even let me attend school. I was her secret and their pet. Used and played with at their leisure.

I lean on the side of the building, reaching into my pocket and pulling out a hand rolled cigarette, lighting the end and inhaling deeply. I didn't even like smoking. I look over at Nina.

"And if you had known I existed, would it have changed anything?"

I look at her small frame, built nearly identical to my late mother. The main difference being Nina didn't look like a walking corpse or have track marks littering her arms. Plus, my mother had blonde hair and Nina's is brown.

If you lined us all up together I would look like their child. The perfect mixture of blonde and brown in my hair, Nina's eyes, my mother's nose. There was no denying we were related.

"Of course it would have!" She furrows her eyebrows like my words are shocking.

"You're my nephew for Christ's sake. I would've raised you as my own. God knows what you have seen and been through growing up here."

I inhale the smoke, letting it roll past my lips as I cut my eyes to her again. I may have only been sixteen but I was bigger than most grown ass men, and I know I was intimidating.

"No, God doesn't know shit about what I saw. God didn't dirty his shoes at the door of my home."

God and I? We weren't on good terms.

I just can't get behind supporting something that puts so much evil in the world. Something that allows for small children to be hurt, killed, raped. If I was in a place of power like God, I think the first thing I would stop was the harm to children.

But obviously he is bothered with other shit, like flooding the earth and having a man build a boat or some shit.

Nina nods hopefully noticing my distaste for her last statement.

"Come back to the states with me. Let me help you finish high school and you can go about your way."

"Why? So you don't have to feel guilty for not knowing about me? Or is it about making amends with the dead?"

I'm being a dick, a certified asshole, but it's only because I have to be. The world chews up the weak and spits them out for the

5

strays to pick apart. I will never be weak again. I will never allow myself to lose my control.

I will never be a pet again.

She sighs, walking toward me, plucking the cigarette from my lips and throwing it out.

"Because you are my nephew, Malakai Adrian. I may not have known you for the past sixteen years, but I love you. You are flesh and blood. You deserve some stability, let me help you."

This would be the time where I should say, if I had a heart, it would've squeezed or skipped.

You see I do have a heart. It pumps blood regularly through my body. It does its intended job. My heart does not skip, it does not break, it does not jump, if it did I would need to see a surgeon because it's not normal for anyone's heart to do that.

It's all in everyone's head.

So I guess I will say, if I had feelings, I would be happy.

My lack of an answer makes her continue.

"The local high school has a great hockey team, I hear you play?'

She would be correct. I wasn't much of an organized sport person, I was more of the brooding lone wolf, but I liked hockey. Let me clarify, I liked being a goalie. I worked well on my own. I didn't need a lot of teamwork skills to protect the net.

It also got me out of that hellhole longer. Away games were always my favorite because by the time I got home everyone was already asleep. Their pet was forgotten about.

"Listen, Nina. I appreciate the offer, but I think I'm better on my own. I can take care of myself. No offense, but I don't need your help either."

I push off the brick wall, jogging down the concrete steps to the sidewalk. I wasn't sure where I was going from here. I had a little money saved, but not nearly enough to support myself.

Whatever I was going to do, I needed to figure it out quickly. I would make it out of this alive. I refused to let this life consume me like everyone else who falls inside of it.

I walk across the busy street to the brick apartments, each one filled with two to three girls, my mom luckily got her own because of me. However in a few hours it would have two new girls inside, probably my age, and they'd have no idea what they were getting themselves into.

I shove the door open with my shoulder, walking up the steps to our 'home' hating the smell of drugs and sex. It makes me nauseous. I step over the takeout containers and clothes. Slowly walking to my room, cringing at the sound of my feet stepping on something squishy. I don't even bother looking down.

I open my door, everything still perfectly intact, just were I left it all. My books are alphabetized, my bed is made, it's all in order, just like I like it. My room is the only one that doesn't have cigarette burns in the carpets. The itch to get out of here is almost more intense than the fear of not knowing what I'm going to do with my life. Anything is better than here.

I dig out an old book bag, shoving my clothes inside as quickly as I can. The only time I am not annoyingly persistent with how my clothes are organized. I grab the pocket knife in my bedside drawer, flicking it open and slicing the mattress open to reveal my stash of money. I grab it all not bothering to count it right now, shoving it deep inside the bag.

I pull a hoodie off the hanger, shrugging it over my shoulders and tossing the hood on my head. I sling the bag over my shoulders, looking at my small room. I was born here. Raised in this room. A nostalgia lingers. It's not a lot, but there's a little.

Before the world introduced itself to me as cruel, when I was a young child, I was happy, I think. My mom would come home from work early in the morning and she would bring me one Mishka Kosolapy. I'd eat it while watching cartoons, then she'd go to sleep and I'd be left wandering around the apartment trying to find something to do to. Then my imagination was enough to keep me occupied, but adults have a habit of taking a child's innocence.

"мой питомец, you were going to leave without telling goodbye?" Her smoky voice scratches against me like sandpaper. I don't reply, talking isn't something she liked to do much of anyway.

Yvonne, was one of my mom's friends, another working lady

and slightly older than my mom. One of the best at her job from what I heard and she made my fucking skin crawl.

Blonde hair, blue eyes, wrinkled complexion, and she wore this cheap perfume that smelled like roses, it would stick to me for days after she visited.

"*Ответь мне, милый,*" she hisses.

I turn around facing her completely, "I don't answer to you anymore, Yvonne."

A twisted little grin greets me as she shakes her head, moving toward me like the snake she is. Like all the other times when I was sleeping. I could smell her stench when she crept into my bedroom.

The cheap silk of her gown as she slid into bed with me. Vomit welled up in my throat, thick bile that tasted like acid.

Her lingering hands lay on my chest, drawing circles, it burns me. My jaw is wired shut as I snatch her fragile wrist in my hand. I stare down at her,

"Don't you dare fucking touch me."

"You're so cute when you're angry, my love."

I have no reason for being here anymore. My mother is dead. I have nothing tethering me to this place.

I can finally leave here, and Yvonne.

"This is done now, Yvonne. You have no hold over me. Find a new *pet.*"

All the nights she forced her mouth on my small body even when I begged her not to. She was teaching me how to service someone, that's what she would whisper. Showing me the ropes.

She made me dirty.

I was seven the first time. My body reacted naturally even though I didn't want it. I pleaded with her to stop, even that young I knew it wasn't right for her to have her hand down there.

I was seven when her pimps came in my room and found her on her knees in front of me. I thought, thank God, someone to help me.

But it was only the start.

They yanked me by my hair, pulling me with them. They took me to the basement where they take the girls who don't behave.

They ripped my shirt off and proceeded to whip me. Over and over again. The leather and glass dug into my flesh. They marked me, because apparently I didn't pay for her services. They beat me over and over until I learned my lesson.

The whips were payment. They got off on the blood, on the pain.

When my mother found me hours later she picked me up, didn't ask any questions, and poured *zelyonka* or brilliant green on it. It's antiseptic and it burned for hours.

I remember praying, praying that God would save me, but he never did.

Yvonne would come to my room nearly every night so she could play with her pet.

I was twelve when she took my virginity.

I was thirteen when they started using me for money, pimping me to other people. Women at first, then it was men. The things they did to me, unspeakable. I wanted to stop, I threatened to tell people at school, but Yvonne told me if I said anything they'd kill my mom.

Last year at fifteen, I became a monster.

They made me break a new girl in. I refused at first. I refused to damage another human the way they were destroying me.

She was young, scared, looking for money, and I could tell this wasn't what she wanted to do with her life. I let them whip my back for hours, five, before I passed out.

When I woke up, it continued until I caved.

I hurt her. I hurt her so they wouldn't hurt me.

I was weak.

I was impure.

A monster.

"You can't leave this life, Malakai. Where will you go? How will you earn money? Let me take care of you, pet," she purrs in my ear, leaning closer to my chest.

Her other hand descends, grabbing my crotch and squeezing roughly.

There was something that switched in me. Like a fuse. It blew, and I just…I snapped.

I slammed her small body into the closest wall, my fingers wrapping around her throat crushing her windpipe. Her shock of surprise changed into a gurgle of air and spit as she tries to gasp for air.

Her head crashes into my wall, and I grind my teeth as I look down at her fearful eyes. I was no longer a little boy and she was realizing that quickly.

"The only reason I stayed was for my mother's safety and now that she is dead." I smirk.

"I owe you, nothing." My grip tightens on her throat, making sure she feels my hatred through my hand.

This animalistic rage surfaces in me, the need for vengeance, to make her pay for every dirty thing she did. To make her feel my pain, every time they forced themselves inside of me.

Her nails claw at my arm, begging me to release her, but I don't.

My free hand grabs the knife again. Holding it to her cheek, pressing lightly. The fear in her eyes grows wider, and so does my smile. A real smile that reaches my eyes, the first smile in years.

I drag the knife down her body, slowly, letting the tip dance along her clothes pressing enough so she feels it on her skin. I release her neck a little, allowing her to breathe.

She chokes for air, gulping it down, until it turns into a sinister laugh.

"You've done so good, pet. Look at the man you've become. Such a good little thing you are. My creation, my darling little boy," she cackles.

I return my grip on her throat, pressing the knife a little harder into her stomach.

"I'm leaving, Yvonne. If you try to stop me, I will slaughter you. I will cut you from navel," I press the knife near her belly button, "To mouth."

"I will crack your ribs open and rip your heart out to keep in a jar as a souvenir. And then as your body lies there, bloody and in pieces," I whisper as my fingers dig into her wind pipe and my mouth comes close to her ear.

"I'll let those special customers of yours fuck your corpse until you're nothing but a home for maggots to bury themselves in."

I release her completely, tossing the knife onto the bed. She slides down the wall, peering up at me with tear filled eyes. Part from pain, the other part from fear because she believes me.

My wrath is strong enough to kill her seven times and bring her back an eighth just to do it all over again.

I grab my book bag, pulling my hoodie back up on my head and move toward the door.

"You'll be nothing, Malakai. Just like your mother, you will be nothing. You're just a fucking bastard."

I want so badly to turn around and rip her throat out with my teeth, but I refrain.

I tear out of the apartment building with a burning anger, rage that scared me, because it was deadly. I could've murdered her, I wanted to. I lost all control and became someone I didn't want to be.

I didn't want to be a monster anymore. Not like the people who raised me.

I suck in the cold air, breath after breath allowing myself to refocus and calm down. When I do, I look up to see Aunt Nina still standing outside the church. I was sixteen, all alone, and my choices were between the evil behind me or the unknown.

I could easily turn around and go back and kill her. I would have to live with her death on my conscience and frankly, she?

She wasn't worth the fucking time.

ONE

Toska

CHARLOTTE

"*I* wonder when we are gonna see the Empire State Building."

A snort of annoyance leaves me before I can stop it. The one time my headphones weren't over my ears muffling the sounds of adolescence ignorance. I have the worst luck.

The pure intellect that my high school is capable of is astonishing. Considering we are in Chicago, and not New York City.

God, I fucking hated high school.

It smelled like dick cheese, Axe, and Bath and Body Works spray mist. Not to mention I'm surrounded by people with the brain capacity of a rock. When did we stop talking about things that mattered?

When did school become more of a fashion runway and gossip hot spot than a learning facility? Was it ever? Did we ever stop shoving information down students' throats so they can pass a test? Did we ever teach?

Where are the classes that inspire, that delve into topics of philosophy, subjects that make you really think, not just remember it for a passing moment.

"Do you have something to say, smurf?"

Oh, original, Stacy. Really.

I'd been dying my hair since middle school, the blue phase never really left so the nickname smurf happened organically.

Stacy, self-proclaimed Instagram influencer and leader of her pack of bitches. The hierarchy at my school was idiotic. Queen Bs they like to call themselves. Their life goal is to rule a high school in Canada, what high aspirations, don't ya think?

I was currently wearing black and green striped knee-high socks over my skinny jeans, I'll let you do the math on what level of the totem pole I was on. I liked it though. Being invisible to the outside world. I was just different enough that I blended in.

Em says I'm Avril Lavigne's clone. He wouldn't be wrong. I think I have a thing for punk aesthetic. The fishnets, the leather jackets, the patches, the music, everything.

"The Empire State Building is in New York, genius," I reply easily.

"How is it that you and Emerson are even related? I mean a man who looks like him, related to you? It's kinda pathetic actually."

I roll my eyes so hard I'm surprised they don't get stuck.

My twin, Emerson, who was blessed with all of the good looks is your friendly, neighborhood bad boy. The title is hysterical. Honestly, it sounds like someone needs to write a Wattpad fanfiction about him. However, it was kinda true. All the dude does is fuck and fuck shit up. Em is addicted to adrenaline, of feeling like he's on a high every second of his life.

There is something about girls my age who love a man with sharp edges and Emerson? Well, my twin was made of edges.

"Well if you'd have paid attention in biology you'd know that when two eggs are fertilized at the same time —"

"I know how it fucking happens." She snaps at me like a rabid dog.

I'm almost intimidated.

"Could've fooled me," I say as I pull my over ear headphones up over my head, getting ready to block out her nasally voice.

"She's just jealous," one of her minions retorts as if it's the most epic burn in the entire world.

There were a lot of things I was. Eccentric, odd, peculiar, awkward, blue haired, irrational, but jealous? I was never that.

"Me? Jealous?" I scoff.

"I play five instruments, my IQ is higher than both of yours combined. I'm a child prodigy, who is a black belt in Jiu Jitsu, and you think I'm jealous of the girl who is gonna peak in high school and failed remedial math? That's a joke, eh?"

Harsh, but truthful. Plus, I may be invisible in our high school food chain but that didn't mean I was going to let her walk all over me. I was peaceful but not a pushover. I was kind of glad Emerson wasn't here, he would've said something about how her pussy stinks and that's a little much.

The shocked looks on their faces amuses me. I'd love if someone would snap a picture and put it in the yearbook with the caption:

'The moment we realized how irrelevant we are.'

"Alright students, if you will head up to your rooms for the evening, we will meet in the lobby tomorrow morning," one of our chaperones says before Stacy can come up with another comeback.

I wave and smile sarcastically at them as they walk to the elevator.

Just one more year, Charlotte, senior year is fast approaching and then you can leave. You won't have to deal with people like this anymore. You are going to leave for college, and be surrounded by people who enjoy the same things as you.

They are going to want to study, to play music, and talk about things that matter. I'm going to have to drag Emerson by his hair to college, but I'm not letting him go straight into the draft out of high school.

If he gets hurt, he's fucked, he has no backup plan, and he is not sleeping on my couch drinking his life away. I want him to have options, because he deserves to have a successful life, and hockey doesn't have to be the only plan.

Instead of going to my room like we were instructed, I manage to wiggle my way out the front doors of the hotel without being spotted. My violin case is on my back, and my headphones are over my ears. I had everything I needed. Today we went sightseeing,

Millennium Park, Navy Pier, Willis Tower, all the things the city of Chicago has to offer.

But tomorrow, that's when the real magic happens.

The entire reason for this trip was to watch the Chicago Orchestra perform. We were a group of band and choir members from a small high school in Canada. Although I'm not sure why Stacy was in choir. I think she likes the sound of her own voice.

I enjoyed anything that involved the violin so I jumped at the opportunity to leave my home and discover another part of the world. I wasn't sure what I wanted to do with my life yet. I was expected to achieve great things, but honestly I just wanted to play music. So I was exploring every option possible to be able to do that.

I walk down the sidewalk a bit, enjoying the fact that the streets are less busy than downtown Chicago, but there is still enough hustle and bustle that I can people watch.

I press play on my music, letting the sweet sounds of Blink 182 fill my ears. When I'm listening to music, when I'm playing music, I'm somewhere else entirely. It's the safest high in the world. There is no place I feel myself until I have my violin in my hands, then I can make home anywhere.

Music is a part of me, deep down in my soul I know that my spine is made of double whole notes. My ribs are a collection of thirty-second and sixteenth notes. My fingers are an extension of the strings on my violin. Sheet music coats my DNA, when I die and they cremate me the fire will crackle and release the sounds of Green Day and the Ramones.

With my head in the clouds, and my mind on music, I don't even notice my untied shoelace. I continue my path down the side-walk, just wanting to walk around a little longer before returning to my hotel room.

I was on the side closest to the road, enjoying the crisp wind on my face when I noticed the large brick wall on the opposite side of the road. The bright colors and striking image pull me in. It's a huge mural, expanding from the top of the building all the way to the bottom. My eyes can't figure out what to look at first. The depiction of the tall man huddled over a group of children, or the war scene that is taking place in front of them. Each piece of the drawing tells a story. The soldiers on one side are holding shields made of feathers, while the man protecting the child has two large scars down his back.

Fallen angel.

I'm so enthralled by the graffiti mural I don't even notice myself tripping on the aglet of my shoelace.

I intake a breath, diving head first toward the asphalt road, hearing the sounds of horns honking knowing I'm about to crash into oncoming traffic.

I tense my entire body hoping that when I hit the ground and get run over it's a quick death.

I wait for the feeling of a rubber tire but it never comes, I'm met with the softness of skin, and the smell of oak and leather. Warmth is wrapped entirely around me, and I nervously crack one eye open holding the other closed.

The first thing I see is the long brown hair and my head immediately starts spinning, my stomach churning.

"Jesus?" I whisper.

I hadn't expected the son of God to look so much like a real-life Adonis.

The light brown hair that hangs straight, brushing his shoulders a few pieces falling in front of his face. His pillowy lips are drawn into a hard line across his face, but the corner twitched meaning he wanted to smile, but refrained. His face was so strong and defined, his features molded from granite almost.

I was swooning over Jesus. Here I am in heaven, freshly dead, just strutting through the gates, and I'm too worried about the bone structure of this man.

Dark eyebrows, which sloped downwards in a serious expression as his eyes ran across my face and body. Checking for injuries, I think. My mind was a boggle of mud, I wasn't thinking properly. I wasn't sure if it was from the near-death experience or how handsome the man holding me is.

There wasn't one feature in particular that made him handsome, but his eyes, they came close. Hazel, but more green. Like fresh dew glinting in the sunlight off a leaf of green emerald. The inner circle around his pupil was the purest form of yellow I'd ever seen, like freshly discovered citrine. For the cherry on top there were speckles of light brown scattered throughout, like stars in a colorful galaxy.

A prominent jaw curved gracefully and the strength of his neck showed in the twining cords of the muscle that shaped his entire body; from what I could feel he had strong arms, bold thighs that pressed into mine as I clung to his wide chest.

"No, they call me Grim. As in Reaper, pleasure to meet you, I've been waiting on you."

He replies with what sounds like humor in his voice, but his face shows no emotion. He swings my body upright, steadying me on my feet. His hands, that are the size of my face, rest on the sides of my arms as he looks down at me curiously.

"Do I need to take you to a hospital? What are you doing wandering into traffic?"

I shake my head, taking a breath, trying to get the world to stop spinning. I can't believe I nearly died. I nearly died and all I can comprehend is that my savior is ungodly tall, like a giant.

I still don't reply, just staring at his eyes which seem to have me in trance of some sort. There hasn't been a moment in my life quite like this one. Boys had never been a priority for me, possibly because I never found interest in anyone.

School and music was my entire life. Even though Emerson attempted to get me to live life on the wild side, I was focused on my future. Boys were not a part of the equation. Especially boys my age.

But this one, this boy, well he wasn't a boy, he was a man. A grown man with eyes that were candidly observant, heavenly, godly, yet there was a heaviness about him. This mysterious, metaphysical vibe he gave off. There was more to him than just looking like Jesus and saving girls in the street.

And my inquisitive nature wanted to dissect every inch of him.

"Earth to Blueberry, what's forty-seven times twenty-one? Can you list the noble gases? Answer anything besides what color are my eyes?"

Embarrassment creeps up the back of my neck, efficiently snapping me out of my trance and sending me flying back into reality.

I step back from his warm grip, clearing my throat with a gentle cough. I see my headphones on the ground and I swipe them up, placing them around my neck once again.

"Nine hundred eighty-seven," I say easily, I brush my hair behind my ears.

"Helium, Neon, Argon, Krypton, Xenon, Radon, and Oganesson. In that order, I can also tell you their atomic symbol, number, and weight if you want."

The first time any emotion passes on his face and it's a little bit of shock. Which I'm more than used to by now. When you're a child prodigy you get used to people being in shock. I wasn't like, graduate high school at ten smart, but I did skip a grade, and I'd already been accepted to Juilliard despite not applying. I was smart in just about everything, but I was a genius when it came to music.

I rock back and forth on my heels nervously. The weight of his presence is like a cloak of sexual tension. My fingertips are still buzzing from touching him. Maybe I did hit my head, because this wasn't normal for me.

"Did you bump your head and turn into Alex Trebek or were you always smart?"

I laugh softly, trying not to blush. He has to be at least twenty, maybe a little older. And I can detect a hint of an accent. It's European, bold, with heavy rolling Rs. Maybe Bulgarian?

"I've always been smart. I'm fine, no bumps or bruises, all my limbs work, see?" I kick my feet forward and wave with my arm. A small grin, the smallest I've ever seen hits his lips, and my heart beats a little faster.

"Thank you for, uh, saving my life, I guess. That sounds like such an insignificant thank you, do you like buttons?"

He raises an eyebrow, giving me a skeptical look as if I asked if he wanted to see my boobs. It's just a button. I roll my eyes, smiling a little. I shrug my violin case off my back, laying it on the sidewalk, and popping it open. The inside is lined with different buttons and pins. I have a thing for collecting them.

I search my vast collection, finding the one I want to gift. I unpin it, close my violin case, and put it back on my shoulder.

"Here, it's my thank you."

I reach the button out for him to grab, which he takes reluctantly. He inspects the pin, a smirk tugging at his vacant face. A bubbly feeling flutters my stomach, like freshly popped champagne, and suddenly I feel like I would do anything to see him smile.

"So a thank you seems insignificant, but an 'I Love Chemistry' button is a worthy trade for saving your life?"

Amusement twinkles in his eyes. He's laughing at me without actually laughing. Great, he finds me amusing. Every young girl with a crush on an older guy knows that when they find you amusing it's game over. They don't find us hot or alluring. They think we're cute.

Like a fucking chipmunk.

"I'll have you know my favorite teacher gave that button to me."

He stares at the button for a moment longer, before shoving it into his pocket. When his hand comes back out, I notice tattoos peeking out from underneath his long sleeve and the paint on his knuckle and the top of his hand.

The graffiti.

I whip my head to face the brick wall covered in the colorful mural. The fallen angel, the children, and the war. It's beautifully done, abstract without being too farfetched, using the correct color contrast. It's beautiful.

"I want my button back!" I shout suddenly.

"That's not how this works. I can't exactly take back saving your life, now can I?" His left eyebrow arches perfectly.

"Saving my life doesn't count if you're the reason I tripped in the first place!" I argue.

I'm joking, of course, but he doesn't know that. So instead of finding me amusing, he now finds me clinically insane.

"I think we should get you checked out by a doctor, *сумасшедшая вещь*," he suggests.

Ah, Russian. I can't tell you what he said to me, but I can break down the language enough to know what he said was definitely Russian.

I wave him off, smiling, "I'm fine." I point toward the mural. "I was talking about the painting, you did it, right? That's why I tripped, I was staring at it."

His face tells me he wants to deny it, and he's about to, until I gesture to his painted knuckles with a bored expression. He doesn't even bother lying.

He looks over at his work, critiquing it without even using words. I do the same thing when I listen to myself play.

Perfectionist.

"It's—" I stop trying to find the written word in my imaginary catalog in my brain.

I look at the man with his missing wings, his back bloody and ripped as he holds himself in front of the small children so they don't see the war going on behind him.

"Toska."

"What is?"

"The painting, it's toska."

I look back at him, seeing him stare at me with a tender curiosity, almost like, who the fuck are you? His pink tongue licks his bottom lips as he furrows his eyebrows.

"What do you know about toska? You speak Russian?"

I shake my head back and forth, I wish. However, I did have a thing for words.

"No, but Vladimir Nabokov said that no single word in English renders all the shades of toska. At its deepest and most painful, it is a sensation of great spiritual anguish, often without any specific cause. That's what your painting represents. It renders all the shades of toska."

His hazel eyes peer into mine, like he's trying to see if I'm bull-shitting him. I have a habit of picking up cool words. I spent my free time in the library or the music room, picking up new words was something I did for fun. If he was searching for answers about my unconventional methods, he would be searching for a long time.

There is a flicker of admiration for me in his eyes for a passing moment, but it's gone as quickly as it came.

"No one's said that before, about my work, beautiful maybe, but not toska."

"Maybe because no one has looked at it through my eyes."

The sun is starting to set over the buildings slowly meaning I need to return to the hotel before I get in trouble. I tug at my straps, clearing my throat.

"What's your tag name? Do you have an Instagram I can follow to keep up with your work?" I ask, pulling my phone out.

"I don't have a tag name, and I don't do social media."

I gawk at his large frame, not because he's handsome either, but because I'm shocked. This talent is unclaimed?

I look at the painting one more time, looking back at my Adonis savior who doesn't move his face very often. I wanted to see him again, when I was older, and he thought of me more as a woman and not a blue-haired child. Maybe someday.

"He's a fallen angel, right? Call yourself The Fallen. It's simple, and you can give your art to an artist. It's a great work, it deserves to be claimed. Careful who you save in the street, the next girl could be a serial killer!"

I start walking backwards toward my hotel, watching as he stares at me with his hands shoved deep inside his pockets hiding his painted hands. I smirk, pushing my headphones onto my ears, getting ready to press play.

"Paint me something one day! Something spectacular! That's my thank you for giving you a name. Don't let me down," I call with a smirk. Check Yes Juliet floods my ears, but I can still hear his voice barely.

"Try not to trip over anyone else's paintings, there's a lot of graffiti in Chicago!" he calls back.

Maybe it was the eyes, or the art, but the University of Chicago just went to my number one choice out of my college options.

TWO

Behind the Mask

KAI

"*C*erberus!"

Get a dog, they said. It'll be fun, they said.

Liars, all of them. Whoever said that never adopted a full-grown male Doberman who thinks he is a puppy.

I walk into the study, which I have turned into a personal library, and he is perched on my leather sofa chewing on what looks like Walt Whitman. Calmly, like he can't be bothered, because he knows he isn't going to get in trouble.

Spoiled brat.

I walk toward him, pulling the chewed hardback book, examining the damage. Leaves of Grass, at least he has good taste in poetry. I run an irritated hand through my hair, squatting down to make eye contact with the black and tan dog.

"You have a taste for first editions, don't you, little one?"

I hadn't gone looking for this dog. He'd seemed to find me. I was strolling back to my apartment after painting a mural on North Wabash when I saw him digging in a trashcan. His ears had been cropped and the wounds were bleeding.

He was rail thin, and it took thirty minutes to lure him into my car. I'd planned to keep him for the night, just get him cleaned up,

23

fed, and then I would take him to the vet. But when I woke up and he was curled at the bottom of my feet, I couldn't give him up.

I may hate the human race, but I have a soft spot for dogs. Plus, Cerberus didn't like anyone but me. We had a lot in common, both of us looked threatening but underneath all of that we had just gotten unlucky and ended up with abusive owners.

I pet his head, tossing the ripped book into the trash. I stand up walking back to the hallway and grabbing the box I laid down. I walk down the long walkway of doors, reaching the end, and open my favorite room in the house.

It took nearly three years to remodel this house. But this room, just this one alone was worth it.

It was a rare 19th century Victorian home, dark green with dark red accents. The designer hated the idea, but I didn't budge. It's what I wanted, The Queen Anne style home was going to be exactly what I wanted.

Custom woodwork including the wooden staircase that showed itself as soon as you opened the door. The outside was old, but the inside was updated.

Victorian style kitchen, with a modern edge that I enjoyed because I liked cooking for myself. The black and white marbled floor, dark oak island, natural lighting.

It was sleek, not those ugly ass rugs your grandma puts down on the floor, but edgy, classical. I loved the balance of old and modern. Windows everywhere let in more light than I preferred, but I could buy curtains.

The outside gave an ominous vibe which is probably why people strayed away from it so much. They wanted their home to feel inviting on the outside, but maybe if they would have taken a moment to step inside, to look around and imagine what it could be instead of what it was. To bring their home to the inside of this house? It would've felt inviting.

All this house needed was some love and although I wasn't the loving kind, I could purchase it.

I slide the cardboard box onto the work desk in the middle of my favorite room.

My sanctuary. Safe haven. The art studio.

I'd completely designed it myself. Every aspect from the second level of canvas storage with a sliding ladder for access, the grey floor, the dark wooden cabinets from floor to ceiling for paint storage, custom lamps and fans, charcoals, spray paint, acrylics—it was art heaven.

And it was all mine.

Hockey was my career, I enjoyed being able to play a sport I took pride in, I made money doing something I enjoyed and that was more than most people could say. But hockey was a means to provide for my other hobby.

Street art.

When I came over here from Russia, it was a culture shock.

You grow up in one place for so long and then you're thrown into an entirely new life. I was quiet, damaged and talking wasn't my strong suit, so making friends wasn't exactly something I was good at.

Plus I wasn't nice.

Not to mention I was huge by middle school so I was quite scary to look at.

At sixteen I was in a new country being raised by a new parent. It was hard adapting.

Nina was a strong, single woman with such an independent way of thinking. She was an artist in every way. A painter, a musician, a photographer, always discovering her next project.

So to help me adjust she gave me her eyes. She showed me how to view the world through an artistic lens, and I've never been more grateful for anything in my life.

I was recruited to the hockey team because of my size, and I had been good, I knew it was something I could make a career out of so I stuck with it. But art? That was the closest thing to love I'd ever felt.

Nina taught me canvas painting, acrylic, water color, charcoal drawing, just about everything she could. But nothing ever struck until I found my bible. My religion.

I was in a bookstore, looking for some new reading material

when I stumbled across *Subway Art, a* collaborative work between Martha Cooper and Henry Chalfant. It changed the direction of my life, forever.

Graffiti.

Some saw vandalism. I saw the voice of the unheard.

Outlaw art. A victimless crime that seemed to fit me perfectly. The quiet kid that scared everyone. It was an underground subculture, an art fucking movement. It was dynamic, explosive, unpredictable.

Climbing fences, making sure you didn't get caught. It was an adrenaline rush that rivaled hockey.

When I first started, I was just following the New York graffiti style, tagging my name on subway cars, nothing too fancy. I wanted to leave my mark, to show that I was here. But then I found Banksy and my world really shifted.

Banksy is an anonymous street artist that started out as a snot-nosed graffiti artist in Bristol, England as a way to shove his middle finger to the British government. However, over time he created a new revolution, something more complex than graffiti.

Street art.

To most it sounded like the same thing as graffiti but it was a beast all its own. With street art you could create murals, bigger, more powerful designs by using premade stencils. Banksy always had political undertones that the masses seemed to understand, people related to. He was changing the world one satirical painting at a time. Art with a message, with a meaning.

The man was a leader of a rebellion. He hung his paintings in the Louvre for Christ's sake and still wasn't caught. He hung his art with Warhol, Picasso, a fuck you to the prestigious art world, and I was enthralled.

It was the ultimate anarchy that woke the world up making it ask the questions.

What is art worth? Who does art really belong to? And who decides what art is priceless and what is not?

I wanted my art to mean something. To capture the heartbeat of society, to bring attention to issues we weren't looking at. Art for the fucking people.

At first I was bombing everything I saw with spray paint, but as I got older, as I studied people like Banksy, Kato, Ben Eine, I started to plan my hits more. So I racked my cans and made outlines. I picked specific locations. I wanted to be loud, but also stay anonymous.

I was seventeen when I painted my first fallen angel. I wanted to bring attention to children in need, homeless kids, orphans, street kids, the ones without a voice. I wanted to be their megaphone.

I was doing it to release my demons, not for the recognition. So I never tagged my work with a name. I left it entirely anonymous. Until I stumbled across the girl with wings.

I was twenty-two, just finished a piece when I saw her flying into oncoming traffic. I wasn't superman, but I wasn't going to let her die either.

She couldn't have been any older than eighteen, and young was never my type.

I was into some kinky sexual activities some might find…rather disturbing, but age play wasn't it for me. I preferred my women to be legal and willing.

Still, there was something compelling about her. Extremely intelligent, witty, funny, and she seemed to understand things on a deeper wavelength than the average stranger.

When I was young, I read all of the Miss Peregrine's Home for Peculiar Children books. I read quite a lot as a child, anything that would help me escape from the reality I was living.

I'd read these books, and when I saw her, I felt childlike again.

She looked like a character straight from those novels, like she had fluttered off the pages.

With blue hair that reached just above her shoulders, knee high striped socks, a Ramones t-shirt and a pair of weathered combat boots. There was no denying just how peculiar she was.

But it was her eyes.

They were an ash grey, almost silver.

Almost as if her mother had stood outside on every single full moon making wishes while she was pregnant. The shining orb had granted her daughter with eyes that were mysterious, illuminating.

Her moon eyes were how she was able to see the world so differently, because the truth of the matter is, the sun? It sees your skin, but the moon? She sees your soul.

Whimsical eyes for a very peculiar girl.

Everything about her seemed different. Like she aimed to be as odd as possible every day.

There are just some people out there who beat to their own drum and she? She was one of those people. I'd nicknamed her the girl with wings because she had this lightness about her, a frail soul, it reminded me of a blue jay.

When she gave me the tag name 'The Fallen' I kept it.

Because for the first time, someone saw my art for what it was.

Painful.

Toska.

So I started tagging my work, every mural I painted after that had my chicken scratch handwriting in the bottom left corner signed, 'The Fallen.' I'd gained quite a following since then, I even once was trending on Twitter.

But the social media attention had never been the goal. It was all about exercising my personal demons. Showing the world the truth behind the curtain of lies. Not all children had happy childhoods.

It'd been nearly a year since my last mural. Twitter wanted to know where I had disappeared to. Some thought I died.

Truthfully, I lost the inspiration. There wasn't anything I'd been sketching that seemed worthy of the side of a building.

I open the box, working on unpacking more things into my new home. The sun had begun to set and I was nearly done with setting up everything.

Until my security system had gone off and Cereberus took off toward the front door growling at what he is assuming is an intruder, but I can hear the culprit at large cursing and I know it isn't anyone that's a threat.

"Fucking eh!" I hear before shit starts falling on the floor and something breaks.

"Motherfucker…" I grunt.

I tear down my staircase, spotting an intoxicated Emerson trying to type in the security code, but failing miserably. A vase I had already planned on tossing out is broken, and he is holding a bottle of vodka.

"When I let you move in, I didn't realize I signed on to be your permanent goddamn babysitter," I scolded like a father to a disobedient son.

To be honest, I feel like everyone's guardian. First Nico, now Emerson. Except while Nico knew his limits, Emerson liked to push far beyond his.

Cerberus is growling at him, snapping and snarling defending his territory. Emerson is slumped against the wall, hands in his hair whispering something about 'good doggie' over and over again.

"Kai, can you get your fucking demon dog? Please? I'm piss drunk and he is looking at me like I'm a ribeye steak. I'm way too pretty to be a chew toy."

I scoff, clicking my tongue, "*Рядом*," I order, which just means heel in Russian.

"It's seven at night, Emerson, on a Wednesday and you're smashed," I note as I walk toward the security system, typing the code in, quieting the alarms.

He presses the bottle to his lips, his mop of curls flopping in his bloodshot eyes as he wipes the excess off with the back of his hand.

"Just a head start for the weekend, pal!" he chants raising the bottle in the air.

Here is the thing. People don't get addicted to drugs or alcohol. People are addicted to forgetting. To chasing a high that numbs them.

I was sick in the head and chose to face my demons sober. I liked the pain, it was a reminder.

But Emerson? There was something he was trying to bury with cocaine and booze.

He stumbles to the couch, simultaneously trying to pull his skinny jeans off. He trips over his feet landing on the edge of the couch with a dull thud. He kicks his jeans off giving me a show of his Captain America underwear.

I grab his jeans, shaking his key out of the pockets. I find my house key and start to take it off the hook.

"What are you doing?" he groans.

"Look at you! You're wasted, your eyes are rimmed! You've probably snorted enough coke to kill Pablo Escobar. Before you know it, you'll be shooting that shit."

He stands up quickly, or as quickly as he can manage, he puffs his chest out, challenging me.

"I'm not a needle junkie, Malakai."

"And being a coke fiend is better? Get your shit together, Emerson, or I'm kicking you the fuck out. You're not risking both of our careers because you can't get your head out of your fucking ass," I seethe with a harshness in my tone that wasn't entirely meant for him.

I'd decided to let him move in when my house was finished. His apartment was under construction and I had the room. Maybe I wanted to keep an eye on him because from the moment I met him I knew he was on something.

Addicts have the same look in their eye.

It's called craving.

Similar to a starved rabid animal.

I'd caught him a year ago at Valor and Bishop's engagement party taking a bump off the bathroom sink.

I'd known he was on something long before, knew he had a drinking problem, but this was the first time I'd caught him red-handed. Anyone who knew me knew my standing on drugs. I made him flush it, and after that, we'd been close.

Close as you could get to someone like me.

As much as people want to think the league screens regularly, they don't. Unless given a reason to and Emerson was too good of a player to lose over a positive drug test.

So they let him slowly kill himself for a game.

Kind of sick, isn't it?

"I want to be better than this, Kai. I swear," he says, sighing.

The bags underneath his eyes make his body look sunken, like a skeleton. The greyish green tint to his irises seems duller. He was committing a slow suicide and there wasn't anything I or anyone else could do for him.

I poke his chest with my pointer and middle fingers, hard.

"Then be better, if you don't you'll be on the street, do you understand? Cut it out on the drugging and watch the drinking."

Tough love.

Sometimes that was the only thing that could save them.

"I'm going to get help, I swear." He nods, sinking back onto the couch, handing me the bottle of liquor.

I nod, not believing him. I believed his actions, but I still couldn't turn my back on him. Because in Emerson I see the person I could've become. Had I not chosen to leave with Nina, I would've been him. A slave to a bottle or a needle.

Maybe all he needed was someone to believe in him too.

I'm going to get help.

Things will be better, Kai.

My boy, I'll be better for you.

I don't even make it into my kitchen before I hear his snore from the couch, knocked out cold.

I empty the clear vodka down the sink. The strength of the alcohol burns my nose hairs. You'd think he was drinking nail polish remover.

Cerberus walks in after me, nudging my thigh. I look down at him, bringing my hand to his head to pet him, as I look into the living room at the sleeping body.

It seemed there was something about me that attracted lost souls.

Just like with Cerberus, I left him sleeping on my bed and never took him back to the pound.

I left Emerson's key on the chain.

THREE

Messy Hair, Messy Heart

CHARLOTTE

I smash the snooze button on my clock, wanting to rest my eyes for a few more minutes. I was in the middle of a very graphic dream about myself and Henry Cavill. The only man on planet earth I'd be willing to do anything for. That jaw could split me in half.

My show at The Cave ran late which meant I didn't get home until two in the morning, and because I needed to finish homework, I didn't get to bed until five.

Just a few more minutes, I tell myself. My eyes are growing heavy once again, the dimple in Henry's cheek is becoming visible in my mind. I wiggle my toes at the end of my bed, feeling my body sink into my mattress as the mistress of sleep seduces me once again.

Until a dreadful sound floats into my apartment. The trash truck is obnoxiously loud at this early hour. My eyes snap open from fear.

The evil truck runs at 7:30 and I have an 8 a.m. class.

Such a doughhead, Charlotte.

I all but somersault out of my bed, falling toward the window. My big toe smacks into the table next to my bed sending a sharp pain up my foot.

"Fucking eh!" I curse as I stumble toward the window, wincing at the throbbing in my toe.

I heave the glass open, sticking my hand out into the open air, moving my arm in a wave motion to feel the temperature. I grab at it like I can feel it beneath my palm. I truly believe my arm is the most accurate thermometer in the world.

Autumn has officially arrived. It's sunny, with a cool breeze that brushes your cheeks giving that pink hue to your skin. Beanies, long sleeves, sweaters and hoodies are finally acceptable to wear out in public.

Which if I'm being honest, it could be ninety-seven degrees outside, and I'd still be wearing a hoodie.

"Lottie dottie! How are you, my dear?"

Pearl, the elderly woman above me shouts. I look up through the fire escape to see her head popped out, along with her tabby cat, Fitz. His head tilts with her, and I have to remind myself not to say something about how absurdly similar they look.

"I'm good, Pearl, just running a bit late, tea and reading after class?" I call back.

She nods with a thumbs up, continuing to water her plants. One of which is a plant called Senecio rowleyanus, or string of pearls which I find very punny.

Pearl is what I like to call a traveling physic. Everywhere she goes there is a pack of tarot cards in her purse, maybe a few crystals, possibly a sprig of rosemary, and if you look deep enough, home-made cinnamon candy without the wrapper.

I feed her cat when she goes to scrabble matches, and she makes me lavender tea that is to die for.

I move back inside my tiny studio apartment, looking at the mess of clothes on the floor and on my bed. Using my superhuman power of organized disorganization I toss together an outfit that doesn't smell bad.

I grab a black cardigan and a grey beanie because I am a firm believer that it makes me look a little more put together. It also hides my band t-shirt and my very, very, pompous professors like to complain about my musical taste. I can't help they listen to Beethoven and I would much rather head-bang to Blink 182.

And it covers my tattoos. The scattered designs of black and grey artwork didn't scream professional, but there was something so appealing about being tattooed. From the moth on my shin, to the winding snake and dagger on my left forearm, all the way to the mandala on my right shoulder blade and everything in between.

They didn't make sense, they were chaotic all over the place with small gaps of skin in between, but that worked for me.

I dash to the bathroom, ruffling my blue hair that desperately needs to be brushed through, but I don't have time to deal with the frizz after I do. There is a blank sticky note taped to my mirror. I look around the bathroom spotting a sharpie with no cap on it.

"Boo ya!" I chant as I pick it up, jotting down a note to get my roots redone because the natural brown underneath this cobalt blue is trying to make an appearance.

Meaning I am looking more and more like Emerson by the day. My natural hair color was a dead ringer for his, our complexion similar, noses identical, but when it came to our eyes they were like our personalities.

Completely different.

While Em's eyes were a dark green mine were void of color, they were grey, a dull steely grey.

I grab my toothbrush and squirt an ungodly amount of mint paste on it. I toss it in the sink as I pop the brush into my mouth. I scoop my messenger bag off the ground, hearing one of the many buttons fall off. I look down seeing it's my AC/DC one.

"Shit," I say knowing I don't have time to glue it back on, but Emerson gave it to me so I can't leave it there.

I pick it up off the floor, swiping my thumb across it. He stole this from a music store when we were ten.

Even then I was into rock music, and he was into trouble. But we did it together, always.

Unshed tears I refuse to cry irritate my eyes. This had been the longest we'd gone without talking. For nine months I shared a womb with that pushy dweeb. I ate all his broccoli and mine so mom wouldn't get mad, and he beat up the guys on the soccer team who called me names. Now? We haven't talked in almost two years.

I know it sounds cliché, naive almost, but there was a cord that attached to our souls. I couldn't feel his pain or anything like that, but when something was wrong, I could feel it in the pit of my stomach. That feeling had become constant since the last time we talked.

Simply? I missed my twin.

But life wasn't simple. Neither was Emerson or our life.

Guilt, pain, sadness, grief sinks into my stomach. Maybe I was being stubborn, but being around Emerson and my mother was worse than missing them right now. I couldn't face either of them. Every time I looked into my mother's eyes, I felt such sadness and all I could think about when I saw Em was anger.

I didn't want to hate them.

So I missed them instead.

I shove the pin into the bag making a mental note to fix it later, and clutch my homework in my hands pushing it inside the bag as well, hoping it's readable. I check to make sure my MacBook is inside there and thankful it is.

I brush my teeth through the kitchen, pausing to rinse my mouth in the sink. I pull the fridge open, noting the only thing inside is take out Chinese food.

Campus food it is then. I really need to go shopping. I toss my toothbrush on the counter, pulling my beanie over my ears, and shrugging the soft cardigan over my shoulders.

"Bag, homework, brushed teeth. I'm forgetting something. I know I'm forgetting something," I mumble to myself.

I spot the black violin case in the corner of the room, covered in band stickers. I swiftly grab the handle, grab my keys off the coffee table covered in sheet music, and finally head out the door. How did I almost forget my child?

My violin, my baby, the reason for my existence in this cruel, cruel world. Okay, that was an over exaggeration but you get it.

As I am locking my apartment door, I happen to look down, spotting my feet with polka dotted orange and black socks on, and that's it, no shoes. I drop my head to the door with a loud thud.

"Charlotte Ophelia Green, I worry about you. Honestly I do," I tell myself again.

I swing the door open, plucking my black rose embroidered Doc Martens off the floor. With my violin tucked underneath my arm, locking the door, I hop on one foot trying to get my shoes on down the hallway. Nearly tripping, Mr. Yarbury laughs at me from behind his desk as I wave at him.

As a third year graduate student working toward a Ph.D. in composition theory you'd think I'd have my shit together by now, but the truth of the matter is if I had to get up before 1 p.m. I was useless. Capital U, capital LESS.

My music teacher from Twentieth Century Music Analysis was going to slaughter me in class, but in my defense I had perfected Igor Stravinsky Tango on both the violin of course, and the piano. I detested the fact I even had to learn the piano. It was too slow for me, too calm. But, I would do anything to get into the Chicago Orchestra.

I don't want to sound cocky, but undergraduate was a walk in the park. My brain was able to work at things I excelled at, and for that reason, I was able to juggle two jobs all through my bachelor's degree. The only reason I'd stopped waitressing and started working full time at The Cave was because they gave me a slot as a performer.

The Cave was a local bar near campus where they played live music. It was a bar for older clientele who enjoyed classical music, a lounge-like aesthetic. It was like being thrown back to prohibition days.

I enjoyed it though. The entire bar was calm, no drunk college kids, plus I could play whatever music I wanted. Now that I was nearly finished with my graduate program, I could confidently say that it wasn't much more difficult. The only thing I wasn't a fan of was the fact people were still giving me absolute hell for being creative. I was bored of Bach, Paganini, and Vivaldi. I was learning composition theory, how to create my own music, and because my music was too 'pop' feeling it was deemed 'inappropriate.'

The closer I got to finishing this degree the more I didn't want to play for the Chicago Orchestra, but it still felt like the only possible way to make a living doing what I loved. So unless the Queen of England needed a private violinist, I was out of options.

When I first went for my job interview, I knew I'd accept the offer because it smelled like oak and leather.

Like him.

I'd been in this city since I was eighteen, and at twenty-three, I'd yet to see him once. I saw his art though. God did I see his art. He'd grown over the years, with his technique, with his message, and his pain. It was like a friend, it grew with him.

There were moments when I would drift off in thought and think about him. I'd wonder what he looked like now, if he had cut his hair, maybe he was married.

I walked down the sidewalk speed walking, hoping to make it to class as quickly as possible. Maybe I could slide in and the professor wouldn't notice I was late. My odds were not high, but they weren't impossible.

"Charlie!"

There was one person, only one who called me that.

I turned around, seeing his floppy brown hair bounce as he jogged toward me. I'd kill for the volume in his hair.

My heart tightened, because I could see the red in his eyes and the bags under them.

Drunk, hungover, or high.

"Emerson."

I breathe out. Two years not so much as a phone call, and now he was standing in front of me. It's not like he had to travel far, he has lived in this city since he was twenty, since he dropped out of college and went into the draft.

Prior to that, he was at college in Michigan. He got a scholarship, and I practically forced him to go. It was only a four hour drive so we met in the middle every Sunday. Everything was fine. We were both happy until everything fell apart.

"Missed you, Charlie. Mom misses you." He shoves his hands into his pockets, rocking back and forth on his heels. I want to hug him, talk to him about how he's been.

Sharp needle pains tickle my throat, burning starting in my eyes at the mention of our mother.

Helena Greene. Or Mrs. Greene to anyone in our hometown, a teacher for all of our lives, single mother since we were three. She was the greatest mother, until she forgot.

"Mom doesn't even know who I am, and you're drunk, Em," I say the words with distaste at the back of my tongue.

Alzheimer's is a shitty disease. I wouldn't wish it upon my worst enemy. Mom was diagnosed at fifty-four with early onset symptoms. Our parents didn't have kids until later in life, so the possibility of something like this happening was increased for us.

By the time we were twenty she needed to be in a facility, so to afford the medical bills Emerson dropped out of college and joined the draft. When he signed his contract with the Chicago Fury, he moved himself and mom here. Emerson was different. It didn't help that right before leaving Michigan he lost his best friend in a car accident. There was something inside of him that snapped; a piece of darkness he wouldn't let anyone try to heal.

I saw her every day for a year, an entire year. Every day. Emerson was partying and playing hockey, too consumed with covering up his pain to be bothered with us.

"You can't still be angry with me over something I can't control! She doesn't remember me anymore either."

"You know what you can control? Your sobriety. Probably haven't been sober in months, I know for a fact you weren't when I was visiting her every day."

"I was busy, Charlie." He sighs, running two hands down his face.

"Yeah, I got that." My voice cracks a little, just enough to show that my emotions are getting the best of me.

Em's face sinks, his eyebrows furrowing with sorrow.

"Charlie—"

"Don't Em— just don't, I'm not ready. I don't want to see you. I need more time." I start to walk backward, needing to get to class, but he grabs my wrist.

We make eye contact and for a second I see the old Emerson. My wild brother, my healthy brother, my happy brother.

"If I could switch with you, I would, you have to know that Char, I would switch."

I can smell the booze on his breath, his wrinkled t-shirt, and shaky hands. My stomach churns, it makes me sick looking at him like this. This isn't him.

"I know, but looking at you." I shake my head. "I can't look at you like this. Drunk and high, you changed after——"

"I didn't change," he snaps. "I've always been this way."

"You did change! You're different. Yeah, you were wild in the past, partied, but you were smart. You weren't on drugs. You didn't need to be high to get through the day, then Ian died and you changed. He wouldn't want this for you, Em."

Fury burns in his gaze, unspoken rage that haunts his soul. He's a slave to the ghost of his best friend.

"It wasn't your fault. It was an accident, Em. You've got to stop blaming yourself."

"Don't talk about shit you don't understand, Charlotte."

I purse my lips, shaking my head with a scoff, "Fine. Shut me out, bottle it up. Keep killing yourself. Real nice seeing you, Emerson. Glad to see some things don't change."

I walk away because I can't stand arguing with him. I hate that there is a piece inside of me that hates the other half of me. We'd been close our entire lives and now we couldn't be further apart.

You can only take so much. So many drunken nights of hearing him break shit. Only so many times you have to open your door to him high. He's my brother and I love him, but love isn't enough right now.

FOUR

Fury Family

KAI

"*I*s there a reason he's getting married in the middle of a mountain? It's cold as fuck outside."

Emerson rubs his left hand on his dress pants, holding a beer in the other. I have a feeling that very soon he will switch to something harder even though he declares he's cutting liquor.

I lean on the banister, retying my bun at the back of my head, even though a few pieces still fall out of the front. I'd needed some air. The inside of the cabin where Bishop was getting dressed was muggy. The powerful smell of commitment and love in the atmosphere made me suffocate.

"We play hockey, Frenchie. You're from fucking Canada, you'd think you'd be used to the cold," Nico chimes in, joining me leaning on the wooden railing, overlooking the side of the lake.

I'd felt it was better to distance myself from all the festivities until the wedding started. I wasn't the person you wanted around when you were getting married, because I didn't believe in it. I also didn't have a filter, so I didn't talk much. Not because I didn't have anything to say, but because I didn't want to hurt anyone's feelings. So when Bishop asked me to be his best man, I tried to persuade him that Nico was the better alternative.

He's been seeing doves and sunshine since he got with Riggs, he'd be Bishop's best bet. However, he insisted it was me that needed to stand next to him on his big day.

The life I lead is without strings, it's lonelier, but it's better that way. I keep my life private. I spend time with the boys, but only on the surface.

No one knows me. Not really. I could be killing people and I doubt anyone would know.

Who I am, what I am, that's private. I release my inner self through art, through hockey, and through sexual acts.

See, I'd lost my control, my choice to choose when I was a kid. My choice to have sex was taken from me, and I wouldn't let that happen to me as an adult.

And now I couldn't have sex without seeing her face. Without seeing the filth she'd left on my skin. I couldn't touch anyone with my hands without hearing her voice telling me what to do. I'd tried in my twenties, but every time I got close, every time there was a willing girl on her back for me, the urge to vomit hit me so fucking hard, I had to leave.

Fully consenting and I still saw the girl's face underneath me.

I tried to not let anything Yvonne had done to me affect my adult life. However, sex was not one of them.

Because of her I don't trust women. So when it comes to sex, I don't do it. Not entirely anyway or in the normal aspect a husband and wife would. I'm not Hannibal Lecter, I don't eat them.

I haven't had penetrative sex with anyone since I left Russia.

I hadn't been inside anyone, hadn't let anyone touch me down there. I finished myself off, made myself come on my terms.

My sexual need was fed by a physiological aspect. I didn't need physical touch. All I needed was a woman willing to be tied up.

Shibari, the Japanese art of bondage. The perfect combination of control and art.

From an artist's point of view, there is no sight more moving. The ropes squeeze their flesh exactly where I intended, and after when I let them down, they will have bruises in certain areas. Across their breasts, their thighs, their ass.

They're the canvas, the ropes are my paint, and I'm the artist. There is nothing on earth more creatively inspiring than the body of a woman. From it come the most tragic pieces of art.

From the point of view of someone who doesn't like to be touched, the ropes ensured that.

I get off on watching them break. After I have tied them up, I break them. There is a point after the third or fourth orgasm, while they are suspended in the air, the ropes I have methodically placed are applying pressure in all the correct places, the toy between their thighs is still fucking them. Their skin is red, a thin coat of sweat lines their bodies, and it's then when I watch them break.

Breaking them is breaking her.

I was a scary person when you peeled back the flesh of my skin and saw what was underneath. My mommy issues probably had a lot to do with me wanting to control women the way I do. Edging them until they could no longer take it was enough to fulfill my sexual urges.

My blood tingles at the image. It's a high, an adrenaline haze when I tie the knot a little tighter, executing the curves of her body, or around someone's throat, commanding their every breath. Their life is in my fingers. They've let their guard down because I know how to make them orgasm, not knowing that if I wanted to, I could kill them.

I wouldn't of course. Necrophilia was a step too far, even for me. What can I say, I'd rather be fucked up than fucked.

That is how I enjoyed my life. Secluded, away from prying eyes, isolated. Now with Emerson constantly stumbling inside, it reminded me more than ever how much I enjoyed my alone time.

I couldn't exactly read while he was attempting to scramble an egg, banging around in my kitchen like a toddler. Then I would have to trudge down the steps with Cerberus on my heels to make him food so he didn't starve.

"What the hell are you three doing out here? What a minute, is that beer?"

We all turn, me a little slower than the other two, until we are all face to face with Nico's ball and chain.

Aurelia Riggs, with her petite frame and icy blonde hair. Her features are sharp, hardened expressions, but she looks delicate with a bundle of blankets in her arms as she rocks back and forth with the baby.

Riggs stomps over to Emerson, grabbing the beer from his hands as he complains, trying to reason with her, but she quickly tosses it into the trash can glaring at him.

"If I wasn't holding my niece right now, I'd kick your ass, Emerson."

She was the epitome of my type. Tiny but curvy in all the places I liked, blonde, successful, bitchy, however, pain recognizes pain.

We both belonged to the childhood trauma club, proud founding members. So that would never work out. How would I help her overcome her parents when my childhood still nips at my heels?

And Nico would've killed me if I made a move. The guy has been a lovesick puppy since he met her. Even though he never said it out loud, the bro code was laid down.

"Is there a reason why Bishop's best friends are outside while he gets ready for the biggest day of his life?" she scolds.

Nico moves toward his girlfriend wrapping his arms around her small waist, looking down at the small life in her arms.

"You look good with a baby."

"Don't get any ideas, no kids for us, not yet anyway."

"Babe, I've got all kinds of ideas on how I want to put a baby inside of you. I've already tried out a few of them."

Nico peers down at Valor and Bishop's daughter, Dalia. She's only a few months old, and she is a perfect balance of them both. Her short strawberry-blonde hair is proof enough of that.

I didn't like kids, but Dalia was cute.

"Barf," Emerson says interrupting their conversation drawing attention back to him and his flask that he is pulling from his suit pocket.

"Do you ever listen? Or do you just enjoy pissing me off?" Riggs says as Emerson takes a sip of whatever is inside the silver container.

He shrugs. "Better than drugs."

I scoff, "Hardly. Come on, let's get back inside. We've gotta make sure he gets down the aisle."

BISHOP MAVERICK WAS a lot of things.

He was one of the best hockey players to ever touch the ice. He was sensible, poised, humorous, a dick sometimes, but he was never nervous.

I'd played with him most of my NHL career and seeing him nervous was unsettling. He'd barely broken a sweat in tied games or Stanley cup finals, but right now, he was a shaking mess.

This is why Nico needed to be standing next to him because he would've said something romantically inspiring to calm him down, and all I'm coming up with is what they are serving for the reception.

I'm turning into fucking Emerson.

So I think, I think quickly about all the pages I've ever read. Every book, every quote, and try to pull the best one. Something that will say everything without me needing to explain it.

Who else better than Leo Tolstoy.

I reach up, grabbing his shoulder, squeezing reassuringly as guests fill in their seats.

"Seize the moments of happiness, love, and be loved. That is the only reality in the world, all else is folly. It is the one thing we are interested in here," I say lowly, just for him to hear.

He nods, taking a deep breath and letting it out slowly.

He shouldn't be nervous. He acts like Valor isn't going to come down the aisle. Like she'll bail on him.

Even someone as cynical as me can realize when a couple is meant to be together. I hadn't been to a lot of weddings, because let's face it, I'm not very friendly.

His best friend was about to walk down the aisle and pledge to live the rest of her life with him. I'm not romantic. I feel like it would be a contradiction for someone like me to believe in romance. I never understood that the universe puts you with one person for the rest of your life, never really found any truth in soulmates, but Bishop and Valor.

What could their love be besides an otherworldly connection?

I'd never found Valor attractive, not that she was ugly, she just wasn't the kind of girl I went for. But Bishop looked at her like she held the answer to every question he wanted to ask. There was no point where he started and she began. They were a constant being. They looked at each other and you could tell there was a secret conversation going on without words.

The leftover snow laid a sheet of white on the ground, and the white covered mountain caps sitting on a lake of pure turquoise set the backdrop of their ceremony. The wooden arch I stood beneath beside the person I'd consider to be one of my best friends. I'd fucked around and landed into a hallmark movie.

From the frozen icicles hanging off Valor's family's cabin to the pops of green foliage they added to the aisle and chairs, even the looming pine trees seemed to have snow laying perfectly, just for them.

The strumming of a guitar began over the speakers, smooth, repetitive. The women in the chairs were already tearing up at the sugary harmony. I stand with my hands behind my back as the sound of a raspy, yet tender voice starts singing.

I recognize the lyrics. I hate this song. It's the anthem for every coffee shop I've ever been to. I lean toward Bishop. "Is she walking down the aisle to Van Morrison?"

He smirks, "My girl has an old soul."

"Not your girl anymore, about to be your wife, pal. Ball and chain forever," Nico says from behind me.

The October air outside was crisp, but I'd grown up in Russia and I played hockey. The cold was second nature. Riggs appears from the cabin, taking her time to walk down the aisle in her dark green dress. I peek behind me, seeing Nico practically salivating over her.

Human connection.

Something that can heal a broken heart and scar an innocent

mind. It's odd watching all of these connections from an outsider's point of view.

I'd be naive to think if I wasn't curious what it was like to look at someone the way my friends look at their partners.

"It's not too late, we can bail," Emerson says humorously. I refrain from slapping him. I didn't want to make too much of a scene, even if he was just being an idiot.

But then I hear a crack of skin on skin, and Emerson lets out a grunt. I smirk, reaching my hand behind my back to high five Nico for doing what I was thinking.

Everyone rises from their chairs, turning to watch the cabin doors where Valor will walk from. Bishop is holding his breath, body trembling.

She emerges from the cabin, walking down the wooden steps gracefully to her father who is waiting with his arm extended and tears streaming down his face. They begin their slow descent down the middle of the row.

Then, as fate would have it, she looks up and their eyes meet. The shivers leave him. He is as calm as the lake behind us, just staring in tranquil admiration of the love of his life.

His eyes are inflamed as he tries to hold back the tears, but I watch two or three fall down his cheeks. It's the only time I've ever seen him cry, and I once watched him take the blade of a skate to the chin. He was as tough as they come, but she made him compassionate.

Valor is red, the color of her hair red, blushing at all the attention and you can see that all she wants is to escape in Bishop's arms. She's twenty seconds from darting down this aisle to hide in his embrace.

She is his soft place to land, and he is her protector. He has always known she belonged to him, and she has always loved him. Somewhere between hockey and heartbreak, these two found love.

More than anything, it's inspiring. That two beings could trust each other in that capacity. I can't even sleep in a bed with someone. It makes my skin crawl, my skin itches considering it.

When they eventually reach us, Bishop stretches his hand to his bride to be and she takes it lightly, stepping up to face him. I feel like I'm interrupting a solitary moment as he lifts his right hand to grasp the one stray curl that hangs near the side of Valor's pale face and tugs on it.

"Hey, Vallie girl," he murmurs.

The nerves visibly lift from her and she has now entered a space that's just those two. The rest of us have simply vanished.

If these two didn't make it to forever, the rest of us could kick rocks.

"Hey, B," she responds.

The ceremony goes off without a hitch, Dalia sleeps soundly in the arms of her grandmother wrapped in a fur blanket, Bishop and Valor cry through their vows, and soon after they are pronounced husband and wife. We are headed to the reception where Emerson can freely drink without Riggs biting his head off.

And he is trying to hit on Valor's step sister, which from what I can see, is working. The kid is smooth like silk. He was honey to flies and women couldn't say no to him.

First dances, cutting of the cake, more tears, and smiles. Love seems to be the theme of the night as the wedding continues without a hitch.

I am sitting away in the corner, observing everyone around me. I don't want to say I'm bored, but I'm bored. Social settings aren't somewhere I thrive.

"Are you always brooding and mysterious? Or is it just to pick up ladies?"

I look over at Riggs, who sits down in the seat next to me, a champagne flute in her hands. My lips tilt into a sideways smirk.

"It's all for the women," I joke, leaning back in my seat, stretching back a little. I'd shrugged my coat off earlier.

"I'm starting to think you're more Zombie than human, Kai."

"I prefer a vampire."

She rolls her eyes, taking a drink of her beverage. She sighs, fiddling with her dress and I raise a suspect eyebrow.

"Is there something you want to say to me, Aurelia?"

She gives me a forced smile, like she's nervous about what she's about to say. This makes me anxious.

"No, I just wanted to chat. You look lonely. You need more human interaction."

"What part of my appearance says I want that?"

I look down at my heavily tattooed body, five millimeter gauged ears, and permanent scowl. Then back at her.

"I have this girl I work with—"

"Not happening," I insert, not letting her finish.

"Kai, she's—"

"She could be Helen of Troy, who by the way, brought the fall of two kingdoms and the despair of two brothers, the answer is still no. I don't do blind dates, and I don't need you getting me women, Riggs."

"You are such a mule! We just want you to find someone. We don't want you to end up alone for the rest of your life."

"If only I were so lucky," I remark as I take a drink of my champagne.

"Kai, we just don't want you to be alone. Everyone else is getting married and having babies. You deserve that too."

"I don't see you barking up Emerson's tree."

She scoffs, "He is young. He still has some time before he is ready to settle down, when that time comes, we will set him straight too. Because that's what family is for. It took me a while to realize that, but this is our family, and you happen to be a part of it."

Family.

That term sounded so foreign to me. Even with Nina, I didn't consider it a family. She just happened to be a great person, who took me in.

"Look, Aurelia. I appreciate the offer, I do, but I'm fine on my—"

A commotion starts near the exit of the dining hall.

"Emerson, you can't leave like this!"

I look over, curiously, seeing Nico and Bishop.

"What's going on?" I ask with pressed eyebrows and a bad feeling in my stomach. I make my way over, seeing Emerson.

Glassy eyes, flushed skin, messy hair. He has a determined glint in his stance. There is no stopping whatever it is that he wants to do. When drunk people set their mind to something there is no stopping it.

"What's going on?" I ask again, but no one answers me. Emerson just continues to fight Bishop off trying to move Nico from in front of the door.

I reach out, gripping Emerson's shoulder pulling him around to face me. I latch my hands onto the sides of his vest, shaking him forcefully.

"Emerson, what the hell is going on? Talk to me," I sound out slowly.

I'm not sure if it's tears or the alcohol, but there is a profound sadness in his eyes.

"My mom is headed to the hospital. She's sick, I've got to go. I have to get out of here."

I sigh, rubbing my eyes, and then rub my hands down my face. This guy couldn't catch a break. Wave after wave of bad luck, every time he tried to get up something knocked him flat on his ass.

"It's a twenty-eight hour drive back to Chicago. Let me help you, okay? I'll call and get us flights. But I need you to calm down, and sober up, do you hear me?"

His jaw twitches, like he wants to argue with me.

"I hear you," he grits out.

I glance over at Bishop and Nico.

"I'll call you guys when we land."

They nod as I guide Emerson out of the reception hall toward my car.

"I can't lose anyone else, Kai. I won't make it," he mumbles as he trudges behind me, wiping the tears that leak down his face away as quickly as they fall.

The saddest thing about it was, I actually believed him.

FIVE

You, Again

CHARLOTTE

*T*he steady beeping of the heart monitor made my head throb. I'd always consider myself an occasional smoker, maybe once every month. But right now, I needed a cigarette. I craved something that muffled my thoughts for a little bit.

I needed to leave this hospital before I go full metal jacket. It's nearly three in the morning and the thought of sleep is far from my mind.

My mustard yellow corduroy jeans that reached right to my belly button were cute with my black turtleneck shirt, but it wasn't the most comfortable.

I was thankful I had the night off already, and even more thankful I didn't have makeup on because I would've looked like a raccoon by now.

The door swings open and in walks my brother dressed like he just came from a mission as 007. He needs a haircut. Those moppy curls are looking similar to Harry Styles.

"How is she?"

"Sleeping, she was combative when she first arrived so they gave her medicine to help calm her down. It knocked her out. It's pneumonia. They are going to keep her for a few days."

He drops his head, letting out a relieved breath, raking his hands through his hair and down his face. I pull a chair next to me, patting the seat.

Our mother was dwindling by the day. Her speech was slurring, her motor function failing, and now she's got pneumonia. With an already compromised immune system, it wasn't looking very good.

This disease takes you so slowly, so torturously that it takes pieces of your family with you. Maybe I was selfish for being angry with Emerson. It wasn't his fault Mom forgot me, yet I was still upset with my twin.

It's easy to sit on the outside and judge me for being angry.

I know it's not his fault that she remembered him.

But every time I looked at Em, drunk or high, I would think…

This is what my mother chose to remember, and this is what he is turning into. Resentment burned in me, something I had never felt for him.

I was angry because why was I so forgettable? What was it about me that was easy to forget and him easy to remember?

He trudges over, falling into the chair with a thud. I lean forward resting my elbows on my knees and looking over at him.

"Who got you to wear a tux?"

He scoffs, "I was at a wedding in Alberta."

A pause falls between us, filled by the even breathing of our mother and the steady beep of the monitor.

It's an awkward moment for us, going from siblings who used to talk twenty-four seven to not knowing what to say. My mind was working overtime, should I say something? Which one of his friends got married? I haven't even met his friends. Should I apologize? Should I hug him?

"I—"

"You—"

We say at the same time.

"You go first," I say nodding my head toward him.

He sits still for a little bit, gathering himself before he begins.

"How did we get here, Charlie? When did everything go to shit?"

When you decided it was your fault for killing your best friend and when our mother forgot me. I think that's when you started drinking, really truly drinking, not just occasionally. Then it was coke. It was just too much for me. That's what I want to say.

"After I flushed the third baggie of coke. When the only things you cared about was hockey and getting fucked up. When Mom looked directly at me and didn't know who I was, and then asked for you."

He looks up at me with tears in his eyes, and it takes whatever is left of my heart. It breaks me. I think I'm gonna throw up. I hate confrontation.

"Then help me. I want to be better, but I need help. I feel alone, Charlie. You're not making shit at the bar. You're barely making rent. Move in with me, we can help each other. We are all we have. It's just us."

I loved my apartment. Pearl and Fitz, even the way my water in the bathroom ran cold for thirty minutes before it got hot. My stuff was scattered everywhere, but it was mine. It was my space to be creative. I loved it.

"You can't just spring stuff on me like that, you're always doing that, just throwing stuff at me and expecting me to handle it. I can't give you an answer right now. I have to think about it." I rub my temples, moving my hands across my face as I let out a heavy breath.

He nods, a few tears leaking from his eyes. I reach my hand over rubbing his arm. "Hey, I love you, Em. Just let me think about it."

He hugs me tightly, pulling me into him. He clings to me, like I used to when we were little. He was older by two minutes and growing up he never let me forget that. He was my older brother, and I was the weird little sister. He protected me from people who laughed at me. He made me feel cool even though I knew I wasn't. I'd never seen him this weak, not like this.

He'd been the strong one, and now it was my turn.

"If I move in, and it's a major IF, Emerson Vincent, you are quitting everything. Cold turkey. I'm not moving into an apartment that smells like booze."

"I'm actually staying with a teammate. He has a house and he doesn't let me have alcohol in the house. He barely lets me have my shoes on in the house," he scoffs.

I furrow my eyes. "What happened to your apartment?"

"Remodeling, I didn't like the kitchen."

"You don't even cook."

"Ladies do, and I like when my women are in a nice kitchen. It's hot."

I retract from him, scrunching my nose.

"You're a pig, jersey chasers don't count as ladies. Does this teammate know you are trying to move your sister into his home?"

Emerson nods, "I'll tell him, he won't mind. The house is the size of Texas, plus he stays locked in his room most of the time. He won't even know you're there."

"I've been here forever, do you mind staying the night with her? I can pick you up in the morning," I ask softly, needing a bubble bath, some time to breathe. I want away from this God-forsaken hospital.

Once he agrees a weight lifts off my shoulders. I say my good-byes, kissing my mom on the forehead and I'm heading out the door before Emerson can change his mind.

I basically skip through the exit doors of the sterile smelling prison and out into the crisp breeze. I wiggle my toes in my black high-top vans, happy to be outside. I was starting to get high off the fumes inside that place.

I move to the side of the doors, stopping to dig my hand inside my bag, feeling around for my pack of cigarettes and lighter. Once I have grasped them, I take them out, pulling one slender stick from the pack and laying it on my lips.

The lighter is refusing to light, so I start to cup my hand around the tiny flame, until I feel prickles of someone's hands wrapping tightly around my wrists.

I automatically go to jerk back from the intruder, but they have a firm grip on my thin wrists. I think this might be the moment I get murdered.

"You shouldn't smoke. It's bad for you."

That voice.

It's a little deeper, richer, but I can still hear the rolling Rs and distinct tone.

I had a nearly eidetic memory, but even if I didn't, I'd still remember him. The one guy, the only person, I'd come into contact with that made the winding gears in my brain stop.

The reason I considered Chicago University in the first place.

Why I followed his work every year after I met him.

And secretly, it was why my heart paused for a moment when a tall, longhaired man crossed the street or stood in front of me in line at a coffee shop.

"Jesus, saving the day again."

A sly glint in his eyes meet me as I finally make eye contact with him for the first time in years.

I'd met guys in college, mostly the tortured artist kind that tried to achieve the type of foreboding charm he effortlessly pulled off. There is something about wanting that kind of attention that gives them away.

It's a sorta standoffish quality that piques your curiosity of an introduction, yet he isn't inviting contact. Nothing he does is with emotion, always with a calm temper and analytical eye.

"Blueberry, still needing saving," he counters, the corners of his mouth tilting upwards just enough to change his face from passive to amused.

Was it shameful to admit that sometimes, when I couldn't sleep and I was tossing back and forth, my brain refusing to shut down, he'd appear in my mind?

His hands, his mouth, my fingers gripping his hair. It built this primal need in me that only happened when I thought about him.

He is an aphrodisiac.

I just knew with every fiber in my bones sex with this man would be earth shattering. Sex in college was fun, I guess. I enjoyed the breathy kisses, the roaming hands and tipsy moans, but I never got to the big O.

Not once with a guy.

I tried, with all kinds of different guys. Jocks, nerds, artists, gamers! I thought hell, they can work a joystick, right?

Not right.

I was starting to think there was something inside of me that was broken. I even researched it. Detailed research. I read books and articles like I had a thesis paper on it. About seventy five percent of all women never reach orgasm from intercourse alone. I wasn't the only one freaking out apparently.

I wanted my toes to curl, back arched, everything I read in erotica novels.

And I knew, this unnamed man, my fallen angel was the kind of guy who knew exactly what women wanted in bed, without having to ask for it.

Because his eyes had touched me in a way that hands could never.

He'd aged well. The slight beard he was growing was trimmed close to his jaw, which was very different considering he was hairless the last time I saw him. Gone was the jeans and black hoodie, he was sporting an expensive black suit that dipped and curved around his body. A pressed button up tucked neatly into his slacks that were trimmed perfectly right above his dark dress shoes. I did see the creeping tattoo that started to crawl up his neck. The black ink tethering with the veins in his throat made chills roll down my spine.

He plucked the cigarette from my mouth, tossing it onto the ground with little effort. I stood there like a dog that just got busted peeing on the carpet. His hazel eyes seem to be looking me over.

"If you wanted to hold my hand you could've asked," I say softly, nodding toward his fingers that are still latched around my wrist.

"Is that so, милая?"

"Does that mean blueberry in Russian, or?"

He lets go, pushing his hands into his pockets.

"If I wanted you to know what I said, I would've said it in English." He tilts his head a little, making his point.

A smile makes my lips twitch, that matches his. Banter was the key to my heart.

I'd waited years to see him again. I should've had so much to say, so much to ask, but just being here felt like enough. Looking at him was enough.

Yet there was so much I wanted to know, starting with his name.

"I'm Charlotte, but you can call me Charlie, Lottie, Char, whatever fits your fancy." I stick my hand out to shake his large one, chewing the inside of my cheek.

"Like the spider?" he asks, not even looking at my outreached hand.

"Like the Bronte sister, and Ophelia like Shakespeare. My mother was an English teacher. And you? Are you Wilbur like the pig?" I poise.

He reaches forward taking my hand, wrapping his long fingers around my pale skin, shaking it.

"Malakai, as in Malakai."

"Your name means messenger of God. Did your mom think you'd be holy?"

A laugh, short, gruff and possibly the sexiest sound on the earth erupts from his chest, and I can see the flash of his white teeth. The way he laughs is like he hasn't done it in a long time. Like it's the first time he's played his record system in years. A lightness floats around in my stomach.

"I don't know what my mother thought I would be, but I know holy was definitely not an option," he says as he runs his hand down his mouth, letting the laughter fade leaving a smile in its place.

"Would you wanna get out of here?"

My stomach was growling, but I wasn't done with this mystery artist. I wanted to know more. I wanted to know everything.

"Are you hitting on me outside of a hospital?" He arches an eyebrow. I think he might be deflecting so he doesn't have to turn me down. I've been through this before with guys.

"A little vain of you, isn't it?" I point out, even though I would definitely hit on him. "I'm hungry, and I want company. I was going to offer to pay for you. If I was hitting on you, Malakai, you wouldn't have to question it."

I mentally high five myself, because that line was smooth. Even for me.

I give him one last elevator glance before walking past him toward my car. I reach into my bag, digging around for my keys as I walk.

"Messenger of God? Really, Charlotte? Could you be any more of a freaking loser, who even wants to know that?" I mumble.

"Is the invitation still open or have you filled my spot with your other personality?"

I stop walking, swiveling around to face him. Not realizing he is much closer to me than I thought. Due to the fact my head barely reaches his chest, I have to crane my head to look up at him.

Butterflies flutter around in my stomach but I continue to keep my cool.

"It might still be. But my offer to pay has gone out the window."

"I'm fine with paying, but I'm also picking where we eat."

"Says who?" I snap my head back a little.

I'd wanted something greasy and by the looks of it, he probably follows a strict chicken and veggie diet. I live off red bull and sour gummy worms. I highly doubt we have the same taste in food.

"Says me."

"Bossy much? Being told what to do isn't something I'm into." I cross my arms over my chest, standing my ground.

With swift elegance, he bends down, until his face is directly lined up with mine. I can see every detail of his flawless skin, the straightness of his nose, the slight tint of his lips.

"I'm starting to realize that, which is why I know this is going to be a terrible idea. Now…" He opens his palm out flat. "Either get in the driver's seat, or give me the keys, Moon Eyes." Waiting with a still glare that makes me anxious.

I intake a sharp breath, holding it in my lungs. I wasn't sure if his statement was more of a promise or a threat. But it made my stomach tighten and my thighs squeeze together. Moon Eyes.

I'd never been called that before. My steely grey eyes had always been boring to me, just two random holes in my face. Yet, he saw them as something more. Like a huge celestial body that lights up an entire night sky.

I pull my keys out of my bag, and drop the keys into his large hand, a hand that could crush my windpipe. He stands to his full height.

"Why is it a terrible idea?" I ask curiously.

He places both hands on the driver's side door, looking down at the ground then back up at me.

"Get in the car and you'll see."

SIX

Her Kind of Art

KAI

"*I*'m not putting that in my mouth."

Well, that's the first time a woman has told me that.

But I guess the chipped black fingernail polish, occasional snort when she laughed and random intellectual facts should've given me the hint that this girl was not normal.

She was smart. Not just book smart either, smart in the way she viewed the world. Always seeing it from a separate point of view. I liked that about her.

She'd told me about the languages she could speak, how she has a thing for remembering lists like presidents, world capitals, dinosaurs even. Her brain was a search engine full of information.

Yet, instead of getting her Ph.D. in something like medicine, maybe becoming a doctor, she was studying music theory. That takes guts to trust in your passion and your talent to give up security over happiness.

"My Russian ancestors took offense to that." I take a bite of the warm food, letting the flavor take me back to Nina's home.

Warm summer evenings or cold winter nights, this was a staple at her house. I don't miss Russia, but I do miss Nina.

She's traveling now, with funds I provided. I'm not even sure where in the world she is, but wherever it is I hoped she was enjoying her time. Maybe Rome, possibly Spain, she'd always talked about Amsterdam.

After giving up her thirties to raise a teenager, she deserved it. She deserved a lot. Everything.

"If you'd tell me what was in it, I'd try it." She crosses her arms across her chest.

"No." I swallow my food. "Then you really won't eat it. Just trust me, Charlotte. Eat it. Don't be so picky," I push, as I place the plate in front of her.

She stares at the plate like it's throw up, scrunching her little nose that has scattered freckles across it. It's cute. She's cute. I hate the fact I find her cute.

This is going to be a disaster.

Because I know that after tonight, I can't talk to her again. It's as far as this goes. I shouldn't have gone with her, but I was fascinated. I wanted to see if her steely eyes still saw the world the way I remembered.

If she still saw me the way I remembered.

Charlotte is young, naive, new to the world, and who I am would scare her.

Scar her.

I would hurt her, leave her messy.

And that's why after tonight, I won't have contact with her again.

She looks down at the food, then back up at me weighing her options before she picks it up timidly. I nod my head encouragingly, as she closes her eyes and does a quick Hail Mary that makes me smirk. Then she finally places the pastry in her mouth, taking a large bite.

She keeps her eyes closed as she chews, her pink tongue swiping her bottom lip as she does.

Chewing doesn't always do it for me, but it is right now.

"Good, isn't it?" I find myself saying as I sit there, eyeing her like a creep.

She swallows, opens her eyes, reaching forward slowly grabbing another one to set on her plate. A sheepish grin on her face.

"Maybe," she murmurs. "What is it?"

"Pirozhki—they are fried puff pastries that have potatoes, meat, and cabbage. This is the closest to home I can get in Chicago."

"Are you originally from Russia or were your parents just born there?"

"I'm from Russia. I moved here when I was a teenager with my aunt. I've been here ever since." I neglect to mention the reasons I moved in the first place, seems a little heavy for this setting.

"So you came to Chicago to graffiti walls and eat at twenty-four hour Russian restaurants? There is more than that, spill the beans. What's your story, Malakai? Do you have four kids and two ex-wives? A sixth toe? Third nipple? Why haven't you done another mural in the last year?"

I lean forward, resting my forearms on the table as I look at her attentively.

Her black turtle neck covers her upper body delicately, showing that her bust was a little more than a handful and her stomach wasn't completely flat. Porcelain skin contrasted her hair and the slightly chipped midnight black nail polish. She had upturned eyes, with fragile features that I found elegant.

She was the kind of girl Hozier would write a song about.

Everything he writes is so in-depth. It's why I enjoy his music. I think he'd see her in a coffee shop, and fall in love with the way that she looked like every season in one person. Summer in her smile, spring in her touch, autumn in her cheeks, and winter in her eyes.

"Seems you have been keeping up with me, why don't you tell me why I haven't painted a mural in a year." I quip, "Since you know so much, Charlotte."

She snorts, wiping her mouth with a napkin. "What do I think? I think you lost your muse. Maybe a girlfriend? The inspiration went away. Artists don't stop creating art unless art leaves them."

I flinch at her assumption. My muse? It was pain, and that hasn't gone anywhere. I'd just gotten better at hiding it.

I'd been sketching with charcoal, messing with acrylics, but there just hadn't been anything I wanted to share with the world.

"What would you know about inspiration, Lottie? Are you an artist?"

I use the nickname as a joke, playfully saying it. This way the conversation is deflected off me.

"I want to show you something, pay, and meet me outside."

"Wait. What?" I call, surprised by her decision. She doesn't bother answering me, just heads out the door.

The fact I'm more intrigued than annoyed is making me think there is something wrong with me. Nonetheless, I wait to pay for our food and head outside into the sharp wind as soon as I'm done.

It's late or I suppose early, but a few people still linger in the dawn. I blow into my hands, warming them up, shocked to see the sight in front of me.

Charlotte has a pair of muffed headphones over her small ears and is knelt in front of a violin case. I believe I'm about to be serenaded in the street.

She was strange, strange enough to play music on the sidewalk at four in the morning, but as she started to pull out the black violin from her sticker-covered case, she seemed at home. Inside the case was buttons, just like the one she'd given me the first time we met.

Every movement went from strewed to graceful. She messes with her phone and hands it to me.

"Press play," she hums.

I look down seeing the song displayed is Galway Girl. I press the button as she says, and it's like I turned on her power button.

Radiance soaks every inch of her as she starts tapping her foot to the introduction of the song, her head bobbing up and down causing the messy waves of shoulder-length hair to fall in front of her face.

Then, she tucks the violin beneath her chin and shoulder. With a deep breath, she moves the bow across the strings producing an effortless sound.

It echoes from the strings bringing a lively tune from the instrument. It's calm, whistling, upbeat. The song escalates and so do her movements.

Her eyes are shut tight which sends vile thoughts into my brain. Leaving me wondering if she'd look the same way, bound and twisted in a set of navy blue ropes to match her hair.

The moon catches the lip gloss on her Cupid's bow perfectly, and she's smiling with that pouty bottom lip. Her thin nose has a slight curve in it, adding to another flaw that makes her more attractive. The next few cords are ripped out of her soul. I can feel them.

They come out so fast, yet so smooth. I'm in awe of how quickly her nimble fingers move across the strings. No wonder her nail polish is chipped.

This is her stage, her performance. I'm just an audience member witnessing her magic. The wind is a paid actor, moving her hair just when she leans back or moves forward.

Her body flows back with the song, the slight bend in her knee, the occasional foot tap with the rhythm, all to pull the lively production together.

She and the music were one constant being. Moving in harmony. Charlotte wasn't just creating music, she was music personified.

Fluid. Powerful. Mellow. Compelling. Healing. Free.

I watched her spin, rock, bend, slow down, and speed up. Following her, every step, clinging to every wafting note. I could watch her for hours.

The passion she let flow from her, so vulnerable, without using a single word.

The tune comes to a gradual end, and when she finishes, she releases a heavy breath like she'd been holding it the entire time.

Claps, loud ones fill the air and I look to my left noticing that this moon-eyed girl had gathered a crowd. A few people had stopped to watch her performance, a few of them tossing a couple of dollars in her empty case.

She rocks on her heels, giving a bright smile to those applauding her. She takes a view and bows laughing playfully.

I'd never been interested in a girl before. Not like this. Sure, I knew the curve of a few women's hips, what they looked like when they come, but this was different.

I wanted to listen to her talk about her dreams, what her favorite food was, and I wanted to watch her play that violin more.

"You're full of secrets, aren't you, Charlotte like the Bronte sister?"

"You have no idea, Malakai," she says with a luminescent smile and a joking tone.

She shouldn't have been attractive to me, but there she was. With her flushed cheeks, euphoric charm, and patchwork tattoos. I'd never found myself attracted to someone's soul, it had always been superficial.

But I was attracted to hers.

She grabs her bag, laying it on the ground, and looking through it until she finds what she is searching for.

"What are you doing?" I ask as she pulls out a black Polaroid camera, pointing it at me.

"Taking your picture!"

"And you're doing that because?" I hold my hand in front of the lens, so she can't take it.

She rolls her eyes, pushing my hand out of the way,

"I'm trying to make a memory here," she complains.

"Isn't it still a picture?" I argue.

She glares at me, slitted eyes, frown, and wrinkled forehead.

I don't like pictures.

But with a sigh, and another swat at my hand, I finally budge. Letting her get an angle she wants.

"When my mother was diagnosed with Alzheimer's, I bought a Polaroid camera and I started keeping sticky notes in my bag. So I can write down things I don't want to forget, and document that I was here." She points the camera at me.

"So that one day, if the disease that holds my mom captive decides to come for me, I can look at these pictures and maybe think, Hey, whoever that girl is, she lived and she had an amazing life." She clicks the button, and I try not to blink. The picture starts to come out.

"Because I want to remember, I want to remember you, and more than that, I want to live."

I'm struggling to swallow properly. Her honesty, how raw and real she is. There is something remarkable about her, more than just her moon eyes and music genius.

The way she is staring at me like she wants me and not just sexually. She wants to get underneath my skin, to see everything behind the mask, and I can't let that happen.

So when she asked for my number before I called a cab, I told her I wasn't looking for something serious. I told her that this was fun, but it wasn't something I wanted to pursue.

She'd said it was something like fate that had brought us together these two times.

I told her that I didn't believe in fate.

SEVEN

Here Comes the Storm

CHARLOTTE

"*T*ell me all..." I hum the lyrics, dancing across the expensive hardwood floor of the hallways.

The outside of this house looked like Wednesday Addams grew up and became a house designer, but the inside was beautifully remodeled and these floors were perfect for sliding across.

I wasn't going to move in, not until Pearl forgot about snicker-doodle cookies in her oven and caught the complex on fire. My ceiling had smoke damage. I couldn't live in it while they were fixing it.

I was stuck between finding an entirely new apartment or moving in with Em.

So instead of emptying out my bank account, I chose the cheaper option.

My room was on the second floor across from Em's roomie. I hadn't met him yet, but if he liked Emerson, he was sure to like me.

I was going to try to keep my messy habits contained to my room. The key word is try.

I planned to make spaghetti before they got home as a thank you for letting me stay in the spare room to try to support my brother in his walk to sobriety. Spaghetti said that, right? It was the only dish I couldn't screw up. And who doesn't like pasta?

Psychos that's who.

I sway my hips, causing my embroidered mom jeans to hang off my hips exposing my black Calvin Klein underwear, but I'm all alone in the huge house so who cares?

Plus the matching bra is the only thing covering my top half, and I think that'll be the first thing someone notices if they walk in anyways. My messy bun is falling off my head as I head-bang through the hall, carrying the last box to my room.

I hated moving, you never realize how much stuff you have until you have to fit it into boxes. I'd been up and down these steps a million times today. I desperately needed a bath to soak out the soreness from my lower back.

I slide the cardboard across the floor, examining the new room. It was big enough for me, but the walls were blinding white, and it was boring.

I'd have to ask if I could hang posters or maybe paint it. I needed some type of chaotic decoration.

The song changes and I groan in happiness. I grab the broom resting on the wall, swinging the handle like a microphone, just as the heavy beat of Diary of Jane by Breaking Benjamin blasts through my headphones.

Emerson said he and his teammates had an event today which meant him and the owner of this house wouldn't be home till later. Just enough time to christen this place with my shit singing and cringe dancing.

I close my eyes, letting my head fall back, and start rocking hard to the deep drums. I was Benjamin Burnley in my mind. There was a sea of punk kids in the crowd and this was my encore.

The beat taunts me, leaving an opening space right before it picks up.

"Ugh," I grunt into my microphone, whipping my head forward and leaning down to the crowd as the guitar hisses in the stadium. I can feel the heat from the lights as my mouth opens delivering the first verse.

The crowd lunges for me, yelling the lyrics with me. I stand straight up, holding my microphone between both of my hands as the tempo drags off, only the sounds of drums fill the void before the chorus goes in hard and Burnley starts to shred emotions out of me as he reveals that he is trying to find his place in someone's life.

"Something's getting in the way—" I roar into the darkness. The rhythm is raging, thrashing bodies, and gritty vocals.

Sweat pools on my forehead and I feel a few pieces of my hair stick to it, but I don't care. When Burnley screams the lyrics, I scream right with him. When the crowd chants my name, I give them more.

The big finish is coming, and all I want is to mesh this deep sound with a glassy set of strings on my violin. I rear back, ready to hit this last note with everything in me. My hand is shoved into my stomach forcing all the air up, as I bend into the microphone.

"So tell m—" I start before my headphones are ripped off my head jerking me backward.

I spin around with an angry expression. I'm ready to chew Emerson's head off for interrupting my Madison Square Garden performance.

"I never expected you to be a lace panty kind of girl. You seemed like the one who'd wear Hello Kitty boy shorts."

Flaming hazel eyes and I say flaming because he looks super pissed. The muscles in his jaw are twitching, lips set in a hard line.

And my underwear is dangling off two of his fingers.

My eyes widened in embarrassment,

"Why are you holding my underwear?" I yell, trying to nab them out of his hand but he yanks them away, closing his hand around the fabric.

"Oh these? This is just one pair. There are four more on my fucking steps," he growls in a deep voice that I haven't heard him speak in before.

I look over at the box I just brought in, seeing the words 'clothes' written on the side. I bite the inside of my cheek, hating that I blush so easily.

It's just underwear? Everyone wears them, it shouldn't even

bother me. But there is something very omniscient inside of his eyes, more than anger. He is looking at me like he is hungry. It's a dark desire that overtakes the entire room.

His eyes aren't looking at me anymore. They are all over my body. But it isn't on normal parts that most guys stare at. No, I can feel his eyes, like he is dragging a pen across my skin marking spots he likes.

My exposed hip bones, the non-existent gap between my thighs, my collarbone, locations on my body I'd never paid attention to he was staring at intently. My heart was beating rapidly. I feel the flutter in my throat.

He was angry, but it was hot.

I wanted him to be angry, but I wanted to be naked. So that he could take out that frustration on my body. He seemed like the type who could hate fuck me through the gates of heaven.

I was lost in a lust bubble, so lost that I was forgetting one important observation.

"Wait, what are you doing here? How'd you even find me? Are you stalking me? Because I just moved today. Are you really a serial killer who has been planning his every meeting with me to the exact second? Is that why you didn't give me your phone number the other night? Because you were going to find me anyway?"

"This isn't Netflix. I'm going to assume the normal option and say you're related to Emerson?"

The lightbulb dings in my head. I'd never asked him what he did for a living, but it made sense that the giant who's built like a brick shit house would play hockey.

"You're Em's teammate?"

"And that means we are housemates. So let's lay some ground rules down, okay?" He sneers, striding forward so he is a little closer to me. This is a different Malakai than who I'd met. The wall built in front of this person was much higher.

"Pick up after yourself, I don't like messes. I don't particularly like humans, but I have somehow wound up with twins living in my house. I have a dog. He doesn't like humans either, try to refrain from getting bit. Help yourself to any of the food. If a door is locked, it's locked for a reason. Do not be curious, Charlotte. It will get you hurt. And as a courtesy," he pauses, hooking two fingers in my belt loop and pulling me closer to him. He stares down at me, searching my eyes.

My mouth is extremely dry, but between my legs isn't.

I know I should be listening to his rules, this is his house after all, but all I can seem to focus on is the demanding tone. The way his black t-shirt fits his upper body perfectly and how badly I want to pull the ponytail holder from his hair to see how long his brown locks are.

"Keep your panties off my steps, the next time I won't be nice about it. Do you want a sticky note to write all this down?"

This felt like a nightmare but at the same time it was almost a dream. This was one eighty from the guy I'd met when I was sixteen, from the guy I hung out with the other night.

I was living with a temperamental, control freak who told me after our night out that he wasn't looking for anything serious and left without giving me his number. And if that isn't humiliating enough, I'd tried to kiss him right before he turned me down.

However, this is the guy I've been having dirty thoughts about since I was sixteen. My imagination was doing all of the work and now he was living under the same roof. Even if he didn't want anything serious, maybe he wanted a sleeping buddy.

Plus he was beautiful to stare at. This was the first time I'd seen him without long sleeves and I had a damning view of the artwork that decorated his veiny tree trunk arms. His left was colorful, it was a combination of paintings by Salvador Dali, Van Gogh, and Claud Monet. They were nearly perfect in the recreation on his skin. The artwork seemed to flow with his body. The other was black and grey, the top half depicted heavenly statues, while the bottom was sinister gargoyles.

It was art on art. And that was only what I could see. I couldn't see his back or stomach, which I know had their own designs. But I wanted to. I wanted to see him naked. Just so I could trace every ink mark on his skin, so I could try to figure out how such a handsome man could be so cold.

His free hand takes my balled up panties and shoves them in my back pocket with enough force that it pulls my jeans down a little more exposing more of my underwear and hip.

He releases the material, his hand flat against my ass and for a moment I'm praying he will make a move. But instead he pulls his hand from my pocket, backs up, and turns around to walk out of the room.

"I guess I dodged a bullet," I say out loud as he starts to leave with a soft laugh.

"Excuse me?"

I sigh. "I just mean, I'm glad you didn't give me your number, or God forbid actually kiss me. You're wound up a little too tight for my taste. You probably screw with your socks on. Matching, of course," I offer with a smirk.

I wanted to push his buttons, maybe see him explode a little, but he doesn't. He calmly turns around with a matching smirk on his lips that makes me nervous. Everything about him is poised, every emotion, every smirk, it's planned.

"You think your smart little mouth is going to persuade me? Make me angry so I'll touch you? Or prove that I don't fuck with my socks on, which let's be honest, you and I both know I don't."

That was not the reaction guys have in the movies. I was expecting to be pushed into a wall and told to watch my mouth. Not this. I suck my teeth, looking away from him.

"Don't play coy now, Moon Eyes. I see the way you look at me. I know you wanted to do a lot more than kiss me the other night."

I opened my mouth to butt in, even though everything he just said was true. Expect Malakai isn't done talking.

"Don't be embarrassed about it. A lot of women want me. The feeling is mutual in this though. I'm dying to see if you fuck as passionately as you perform, but I'm not going to do that. You wanna know why?" he asks.

Liquid heat leaks between my legs at his confession. So obviously he'd been watching me for a lot longer than I knew. I rocked on my heels, not being able to stop myself from saying,

"I don't, but I'm sure you're going to tell me." I cross my arms over my chest, attempting to show that I'm unaffected by his words.

He chuckles, it's deep, masculine, and I can only imagine what it sounds like when he just rolls out of bed.

"Because I have self-control, which is something you lack. You're a smart girl, Charlotte. Smart enough to know that I'm your brother's friend, and I'm not going to disrespect him by sleeping with you. I don't need him jumping down my throat after I fuck you and you're heartbroken because I don't want to go on a date or cuddle. So I won't be touching you. Even if you intend on wearing that..." He looks me up and down.

"Around the house."

With one last fleeting glance, he walks out of my room, shutting the door behind him.

Malakai was a storm. A raging hurricane, a monumental wave of mystery and trouble. A thunderstorm of intelligence and darkness. He was right. He was my brother's friend, and I did lack self-control. He was right when he said we wouldn't work out the other night. But what he didn't know is that:

I never minded a little rain.

EIGHT

Team Meeting

KAI

I'd once read a quote and it said,
"Some people are artists. Some of them are art."
And Charlotte was a Jackson Pollock.

Because she was a mess, but somehow she ended up beautiful and sold for half a million dollars. She had splashy lines and purposeful yet accidental paint drops. Intentional messiness.

Living with her was living with a fucking tornado.

Walking by her room during the day made me want to call a cleaning service. Clothes were thrown around, pairs of headphones laid out with records underneath them. Her record player was on the floor instead of the dresser. Don't ask me why. And the sheet music...

It. Was. Everywhere.

Piece after piece of sheet music covered the floor, her bed, her desk. It was an optical illusion of lines and notes.

I'd watched her stumble out of her bed late, as customary. I don't think she ever made it to class on time. She'd nearly tumbled down the steps trying to put her shoe on, and each day her outfits got more creative.

Jeans with threaded messages on the back pockets, not that I

73

read them of course, because then I would be staring. Embroidered jean jackets, fishnets beneath shorts, and the unmatched socks. God they drove me wild.

They always came to her knees when she wore skirts or shorts, and there was something very naughty schoolgirl about it.

I'd given in the other night when I heard her playing. Given in to her temptation.

I thought having a musician next door would irritate me at night because that's when I work in my room, but it was the opposite.

My studio was right next to her room, so I could hear the metallic, vibrant tones through the wall. Moon Eyes seemed to have insomnia, and she dealt with it through the violin. I could always tell when she had a good day versus a bad day which was leaving an impression on my art.

If the cords she played were deep, dark, muted, more veiled than airy, she had a bad day. If it was flute-like, wafting, sweet, and pure, she had a good day. I could feel her emotions, each time her bow moved it let out how she felt.

Depending on which she executed determined the kind of art I was creating. Bad days meant I used less color; the opposite was a vast array of colors. I was letting her bow across the strings guide my brush.

But the other night, I'd seen her through the crack of her door. Sitting on the floor with a white t-shirt on. I could see her silky skin and the black panties that barely covered her round ass. Her body swayed back and forth to the melody, eyes sealed, and her recently dyed hair swirling everywhere.

My dick was pressing against my zipper, angry, hot, pissed. That had never happened before, not without tying someone up first. Yet all it took was my eyes spotting the silhouette of the piercings that were in her perk nipples.

I had to turn around and head to my shower. I couldn't recall the last time I'd gotten hard just looking at someone, but there I was in my shower thinking about her with my cock in my hand.

And it was just her. There were no intrusive thoughts of my

past, just her skin, her laugh, her slightly crooked nose, pouty lips, and those eyes.

She made me do a lot of things I wasn't comfortable with, things I'd never done before. So I tried my best to make sure we ran into each other as little as possible.

I was gradually getting used to the sticky notes around the house that had reminders on them, but what I was never prepared for was the fact she played mean.

Leaving her underwear on the steps every once in a while. A game she liked to play because I told her no. I would scoop them up, hoping her brother hadn't stumbled upon them before I did, and shove them into my pocket.

I was growing a collection of Charlotte's panties in my room, but I wasn't going to give her the satisfaction of giving them back, so I just kept them.

Secretly I liked it, how she seemed innocent with her rosy cheeks, but she was mischievous enough to leave underwear on the steps just for me. So I would know she was thinking about me.

Like the ones I forgot to put into the drawer in my room, the ones that are still in my back pocket as I walk into the locker room for practice.

The same silk purple panties that just fell out of my pocket while I was changing and are currently in Nico Jett's hand.

"Malakai Petrov, purple is definitely your color."

I grab them from him. Glad that no one else is paying attention and pissed he was holding her underwear. If I blushed, now would be the time I'd do it.

I shove them into my bag, zipping it up so no one else can see it, and I continue to get dressed for practice. Except Nico is staring at me like a bored housewife waiting for me to spill all the gossip.

"Are you going to tell me who owns them? Or am I going to have to assume you are a crossdresser? I mean I love you, either way, I'm just saying—"

"Nico, shut up," I grunt.

"So there is someone?" he pushes.

Not exactly. Just a blue fairy that is taking over my house.

"Who are we talking about?" Emerson announces as he walks toward his locker.

Even though they were twins, Emerson and Charlotte didn't look alike. Which had to do with the fact boy and girl twins don't ever look that much alike. Or maybe I was trying to convince myself that I wasn't attracted to Emerson.

But the way they interacted you could tell they were siblings. She took care of him, making sure he ate, that he had clean clothes. I hadn't seen him drink since she moved in.

But I know addicts and they can be sneaky. His skin had more color and his eyes weren't always so red. The coke had made his hockey ability jittery, but also it made him amped up. He played with such ferocity it was scary.

I just hope sober Emerson doesn't feel the urge to use because he thinks it makes him better.

"Kai had panties in his pocket and he won't tell me whose they are. You live with him, is there anyone he is sneaking out?"

Reason number one I didn't enjoy having friends, they always want into your business. I liked my private life exactly how it was, private.

"The only chick in the house is my sister and he isn't her type. Other than that he's been celibate from what I have seen. It's kind of sad," Emerson answers coolly, pulling his shirt off.

"I don't need a new pussy every day to be satisfied, you walking STD."

I keep a straight face, lucky I rarely show emotion. I'm not scared of the kid, but I'm not in the mood to fight anyone over someone I hadn't even had sex with.

Wait, not her type?

"I wouldn't want my sister near a serial killer, he might eat her."

Emerson laughs, "Charlie usually goes for guys with a little more life about them. No offense, Kai, but you remind me of a corpse."

I force a tight-lipped smile.

A corpse who makes your sister's panties wet.

"None taken. She isn't my type either, so no worries. Nico, keep your nose in your own sex life."

I start pulling on my pads, getting ready to sweat for the next two hours. I loved my job, I loved being a goalie. I could go onto the ice and blank out for a few hours. I wasn't thinking about anything, just relying on instinct and my body to know what to do when the time was right.

Charlotte likes lively guys? I don't see her being the type to date the captain of the football team or the golden boy. There isn't any type of guy I see her with actually. She's too unique. There is so much of her to take in, I don't think any guy is capable of really appreciating it.

I'd found her yesterday reading my Van Gogh book onto the counter while feeding Cerberus peanut butter on a wooden spoon. I don't know another girl like that.

Which was another thing that pissed me off, Cerberus loved her. We were supposed to be human haters together and then a pretty girl walks in and he becomes a traitor.

"Since I have you both here, Riggs has been up my ass about making sure this Christmas game happens. She and Valor want to make it an annual thing. It'll be two days into our holiday break and you have to be there or she is going to scalp me," Nico says as he shrugs his jersey over his shoulders.

"Who is going to be there?" Emerson asks.

"Us three, Riggs, Valor, Bishop, Valor's dad, and his new lady friend. Then, of course, Dalia who isn't going to be hitting the ice at five months old."

I lace my skates, grabbing my phone, and typing the event into my calendar app so it reminds me.

"Valor's dad? As in JR Sullivan?"

"The one and only," I reply to Emerson.

"Can the dude still skate? I mean I don't want to break a legend's ankles."

Nico laughs hard, holding his belly and I snicker along with him.

JR Sullivan might have been older, but it didn't mean the talent left him. The man was in the Hockey Hall of Fame for a reason.

"JR is going to skate circles around you, Frenchie, and I for one can't wait to see it happen." Nico slaps his back heading out of the locker room toward the practice rink.

I finish getting all of my shit on, grabbing my glove and stick when Emerson stops me.

"Could you pick Charlie up from work? I have a date and her car is in the shop."

Every time I try to stop thinking about her, someone keeps reminding me of her name. All I seem to do anymore is think about her and how she makes everything in my fucking house feel so alive.

"Yeah, I will. But, Emerson," I start.

"Don't come home drunk, she waits up for you, all night. She knows when you smell like booze. I don't feel like waking up to you two arguing," I finish.

He nods, chewing his bottom lip anxiously,

"I know she worries, but I'm not drinking tonight. I've been sober since she moved in. Scout's honor," he says with a light grin, holding up three fingers.

An addict isn't an addict until they lie to you.

NINE

Foreigner's God

CHARLOTTE

"I'm not saying we aren't going to win the cup this year. I'm just saying Greene is inconsistent and Petrov is getting old. He has given us great minutes in the goal, but it's time to trade or for him to retire."

"Petey, that's a little pot calling the kettle black, don't ya think? You're no spring chicken either. Nico Jett is only a few years younger than Kai and he is playing just fine, leading the league in power-play goals at that."

I love watching older men talk. Especially these two. Fred and Pete were regulars, one ordered a Tom Collins with a double shot of gin, and the other ordered a Manhattan. They were in their late seventies and had served in the military together.

Pete leans in close to him, "No, Freddy, but I know when to call a spade a spade, and Petrov is too old to be our number one guy in the goal."

I slide their drinks to them.

"Boys, since when is twenty-nine old? What would that make you, fine gentlemen, ancient?" I ask with a raised eyebrow and a smirk.

"Charlie, that makes you way too young. What are you now,

twenty-one? And what are you doing, reading up on hockey players lately? Is that the new list you're memorizing?" Pete questions as he mixes his drink that I have already mixed.

"No, I'm actually trying to learn Russian right now. So I'm not learning any new lists and I watch hockey!"

They give me a bored look, and at the same time say, "Since when?"

I shrug, "Like two days ago."

Which is true! It's maybe hard to believe but when it came to hockey, I didn't know a lot. I never really went to Emerson's practices or games, because I had practice or a recital. We were on opposite schedules in high school. I made it to a few games in college, but it was just a bunch of boys skating back and forth chasing a tiny ass puck.

I'd watched my first game two nights ago because the house was empty, and I was bored. So I clicked the TV on and watched the entire game. They won, and apparently, Kai had what I think is called a shutout, which I Googled and saw it meant he didn't let anyone score.

He looked so much smaller on the screen, but he moved so quickly. You'd think his reflexes would suck because he is so big, but it's the opposite. He is extremely agile, his head moves so fast making sure his eyes always stay on the play.

I would agree with the men in saying Emerson was inconsistent. In the beginning, he was on fire, had two goals in the first half, then he dwindled off, and not just from being tired. There was something else about it.

"Exactly, us old men have been watching hockey before you were born, Charlie."

I roll my eyes, finding it comical that they were talking about people I knew. Neither of them knew who my brother or our roommate is.

"You're worse than women," I mutter jokingly as I wipe the bar off. I had another hour and a half on this shift, and the last thirty minutes I got to play music, which was the only reason I stayed here.

To play music. I didn't have to play classical music or listen to someone lecture me for an hour about my finger placement.

Lately, the music I've been playing has been a little slower, a little more sensual because he likes to watch me, or listen at least.

He thinks I don't know, but we live in an old house and the floorboards creak every time someone breathes. Even though he thinks he is invisible. I can still see him through the crack in my door at night when he should be asleep, not watching his best friend's sister.

There is a part of me that thinks even when he isn't watching, he is listening, somewhere in the house so I play for him and when I play for him it always seems to have a sexual feel. Or maybe it's just me.

Me imagining that when I shut my eyes it's just us and he is the guy I met before, the one who didn't avoid me. The one who called me Moon Eyes.

"Charlie! You have someone asking for you, booth three." One of the other waitresses shouts, and I nod leaving my spot behind the bar to navigate the main floor in front of the stage. I swing around the front of the booth.

"Welcome to the Cave, what can I get for—Malakai?" I ask, laying eyes on the one person I never expected to be in here.

The shadows hide pieces of him, making him hard to see, but the dim lights catch the sliver ring tracing circles on the rim of his glass. He sits leaned back into the darkness like a predator gazing for prey.

"Why are you working in a bar that looks like it was made during the same time the Berlin wall was standing?" His gravelly voice echoes inside my chest, warming my body up. There was something sexy about this. Something forbidden, something lustful between us.

I cross my arms over my chest. "Better question! What are you doing here?"

"Your brother had a date, and I had to pick you up. Consider me your chauffeur," he says in a bored tone as if he would rather be anywhere else but here.

"I try not to consider you at all," I snip. After our first day roomie meeting I wasn't playing nice either.

"My shift isn't over. I go on in a few minutes so you can leave, and I'll get a cab," I add, not wanting the pressure of him being here when I play.

"Or, I can just wait?"

"Or, you could just leave."

"Why do you want me to leave so badly? You don't want me to watch you perform? I've seen it before. Do I make you nervous, *Charlotte*?" A grin pulls at his lips, I can see his white teeth gleaming and something tingly settles in my stomach.

The way he says my name is the same way I imagine he would say the word *pussy* or *cunt*. It's low, gritty, and it's nearly a whisper like he said it in my ear while he was on top of me, inside of me.

"You don't make me nervous. You piss me off, and I don't like playing when I'm angry."

He laughs like I'm a joke, like all I am is his friend's sister. Like he doesn't take me seriously.

"I make you something, just like you make me. So, why don't you go up there and show me? Lay all your cards out on the figurative table, if you will."

I bite my bottom lip, swallowing gently. My skin burned like someone had turned the temperature up a few degrees. My fishnet knee highs were feeling remarkably tight, my skirt a little too short.

"I don't think you want me to do that," I warn, tapping my foot nervously.

"Oh? And that's because?" I can practically hear him lifting his eyebrow.

I bend a little, placing my palms on the table and inclining into his space more. It's unnatural how the air changes when I'm close to him. I've felt that way since the first time I'd met him. Like I entered a new world when I was near him.

Everything he did seemed to be other worldly. He was disconnected from the world. I wanted to be in that world with him. The way he walked around the house, how he cared for Cebby, (he hated that nickname for the dog,) or when I see him extended on the couch reading.

Sometimes it's in English, other times he reads Russian. Tolstoy, Twain, Faulkner, Austen, he reads it all. I could watch him flip pages for hours, he takes no longer than three minutes on a page. He wrinkles his forehead when he rereads something he didn't understand. And he puts his fist in front of his mouth so he can hide his smile when he reads something he likes.

I've seen him disappear into his studio, but it's always locked. I've tried every bobby pin in the house, it won't open. I know that's where he keeps his art, where he works, and according to Emerson, where he takes his lady friends.

My curiosity kills me at night. Is there a bed in there? A chain wall? With all the spare bedrooms why does he mix his pleasure with his art, unless they are the same. When I'm supposed to be studying, I have my fingers between my pale thighs dancing to thoughts of what he looks like in his room. Shirtless, bent over a painting that has taken days to finish, frustrated when it doesn't come out correctly.

Creating art looking so damn much like art itself.

If that's true, I want to be his muse. Just to know what it feels like to be with him. To touch him, to be touched by him.

"Because I could burn this place to the ground with what I feel for you, but you're afraid, Malakai," I answer truthfully.

He leans onto the table, suddenly, elbows resting on the wooden surface, his face coming into the light a little more. I gasp louder than I wanted to, but I can't help it.

His hair is down.

Falling just a little past his shoulders in soft brown waves. They frame his angular face but it's not too much, the hair isn't overwhelming him if anything it's making him stand out more. I wonder if it's as soft as it looks. I'd never gone for guys with long hair. Mostly because they either looked homeless or were homeless.

After seeing him with his hair down, I planned to steal all the hair ties in the house and burn them. He was no longer allowed to wear it in a bun. I forbid it.

"Afraid of you? The five foot nothing twig that I could snap in half if I wanted to?" he retorts.

I click my tongue a few times, shaking my head. "Threats, threats, that's all you do is talk. The truth is you won't touch me because I scare you. The six-foot-something giant that I could break if I wanted to."

He scoffs, moving so that our faces are close. Closer than they have ever been. I flick my eyes to his lips for a brief moment, catching his tongue run across his bottom one. Then I'm back to his hazel eyes, flaming yellow.

"You're a brave little thing coming at me like this."

My stomach quivers as my thighs shake, his words, the way he says things sends my body into a frenzy. Every word sounds like a grunt, like he is groaning them into my skin while he's inside of me.

"Just a girl who knows what she wants," I whisper with what scarce confidence I have left.

I think I have won this banter battle; I've succeeded in outwitting him. Except I'm not. Kai is always two steps ahead of me and I suck at chess.

His left hand raises to my cheek and I flinch a little when he makes contact with my skin. With his thumb, he brushes back and forth leisurely on my cheek bone as he gazes at me. Then like a switch the same hand fastens onto the back of my neck with a scary force. It makes my elbows bow and the table rattle.

Our noses are touching and his breath is kissing my lips. He tilts his head to the left a bit, less than an inch and I'd be kissing him. Those lengthy fingers dig into the surface of my neck pinning me. He inhales through his nose, sniffing me, drinking me in like he can't get enough of me.

Liquid heat flows between my thighs, proving to me just how much I like him. I'm never this wet, not even during sex. He has barely touched me, and I'm like Niagara Falls.

My tongue passes over my dry bottom lip, grazing his in the process. I can taste the leftover vodka on him as if I'm not drunk enough on him. He groans lowly, clutching me tighter.

"You want me, Moon Eyes? Prove it. Show me how bad you want me and maybe, if I'm impressed, I'll consider it."

My body throbbing hard, my heart pressing against my throat obstructing me from replying.

Malakai was always calculated, always organized, and I wanted to make a mess of him. Muddy him up until he was so lost in me, he'd never find his way out.

TEN

Bringing Heaven to You

KAI

*T*he small bar was nestled in the middle of nowhere. Some would call it quaint, a hole in the wall. The old school speakeasy meets mid-century vibe resonated through the mahogany bar at the back of the room, a stopping point to the main event.

The signature red leather booths scattered across the main floor of the lounge created a semi-circle around a small stage with black satin curtains. Everyone in here was either born in the century this kind of lounge was cool in, or looked like they were traveling and accidentally found this on Google.

I was still fiddling with my first drink, sitting uncomfortably in my jeans that felt a lot tighter since leaving practice.

Fucking Charlotte.

Charlotte and her short skirts and fishnets.

Charlotte and her ratty Dead Kennedys shirt that seems molded to her body due to how often she wears it.

Charlotte, Charlotte.

I wanted her out of my house. I needed her out of my house for the sake of my sanity. If she didn't move, I was going to have her in my bed, and that situation leads to nothing but a dead end.

She'd end up in my bed, legs spread, looking like an angel, and I'd be dying to be inside of her.

Then I'd hear it.

I'd hear Yvonne's voice crawl up my spine.

"Pretty, little pet, take her."

I wouldn't be able to focus on Charlotte. Not the way she deserves to be focused on. I hated my past for still having chains wrapped around me, holding back from experiencing certain things.

I tie them up so they can't touch me. So they will never be able to touch me again. I use toys so I never have to scar another human.

How screwed up do you have to be that all you need to get off is watching women struggle in ropes you've tied them in?

Charlotte didn't deserve that. She deserved a man who could make love to her. Who could have sex with her and not picture their abuser.

But she was making me want to fuck her.

She was forcing me to feel this hunger in my stomach that made my dick want to see what it was like to be inside of her.

Lust filled, wicked sex. I wanted that with her, but it was something I was never going to have. Yvonne ruined that for me a long time ago.

Her being in the house was forcing me to imagine what she tasted like, making me think about what she sounds like when she needs air, forcing me to think about what she feels like when she wants to come.

This was all her fault, her fault for making me want things I could never have.

Moon Eyes takes her place center stage, looking out into the crowd, smiling softly, a light blush on her cheeks when her eyes inevitably land on me.

I wonder if she blushed with her entire body.

Those pretty little eyes that stare right through me. My dick jerks at her arrival. It's becoming irritating how he reacts when she is around. I'm starting to think she has a remote controlling him, because it only happens around her.

I watch the vein in her neck pulse, not because she is nervous, but because she's turned on.

This performance may be in public, but it was for me.

It was her and I, alone in this room.

She liked my attention. It's why she leaves her panties on my steps because she wants me thinking about her.

She has it now, my undivided attention, and I'm eager to see what she is going to do with it.

I nod my head as if to say, "Go ahead, give me all you got."

Only when the music plays over the speakers do I notice she doesn't have her violin. It's just her and a microphone.

The soulful rock beat matches her foot tapping as the introduction of drums and guitar blend together just in time for her to open her mouth.

"Stranded in this spooky town..." she sings into the microphone, her whiskey-coated voice pervades the space like smoke. It's husky in all the right places and soft in parts, you wouldn't expect.

My fingers grip the glass tighter, if not, I would have done something idiotic like yank her off the stage and onto my lap.

She eases up through the first verse, leaving breathy vocals that have me readjusting myself. Then the chorus comes in sultry and heavy. The drums drop just as she swings her hair forward.

"I see a storm bubbling up from the sea..." she groans, swaying her body forward with a vigorous push.

"Fuck," I mutter, as one hand runs down her body sensually, outlining her curves showing me precisely where she wants me to touch her.

I wonder if she feels the vibrations of the music between her thighs, rocking back and forth like she's sitting on my face ready to come at the flick of my tongue.

If her adrenaline is pumping the way mine is as she wrinkles her forehead and shuts her eyes making me wonder if that's what she will look like trying to fit my cock inside of her.

There was electricity, a spark that resonated between us, every lyric was pulled from a place of deep yearning. She was aching for me, begging me to touch her and this was her final plea.

She's in control right now. Her body owned the rhythm and the pace. I was letting her fuck me and I couldn't do anything about it but watch and try not to come.

The guitar solo hisses into the darkness as she tries to catch her breath, bending her head down for a moment before she looks up making direct eye contact with me and her lips start moving again.

The bright lights show me the sweat that is making her hair cling to her forehead, her flushed skin, and her heaving chest.

It's slow at first, until the beat climaxes and she has her hand on her stomach pressing so that she can deliver everything she has to these notes. So she can give everything to me. The last few words are ripped out of her soul.

"And it's coming closer!" she whines out with so much passion in her tone that it's physically impossible for me not to feel it.

I lift the glass to my lips, downing the watered-down vodka and standing up as the crowd claps for her.

I roll the sleeves of my long sleeve shirt up as I storm toward where I saw her disappear to earlier. The backstage door with the words Employees Only is clear, but I couldn't give a fuck.

I need to be touching her. I wanted her tied up, dangling, with a vibrator between her thighs screaming as she orgasmed, and I painted her at her most pleasurable moment.

I look around the space, spotting her stumbling through the curtains leaning on the exposed brick for support as she holds her chest.

"Give them to me," I growl with a voice I've never heard before.

"I'm sorry?" she asks, trying to gather herself.

I stalk in her direction making her back up into the brick. I place my palm on the brick and I hold the other out to her,

"Your panties, Charlotte, hand them over." I flick my middle fingers at her.

Her mouth pops open and her eyes widen, shocked at my demand, but she's intrigued. She isn't sure if she is more turned on or embarrassed.

"What if someone comes in? Or hears me, Kai?"

I squint my eyes, snapping, "Do I look like I give a fuck right now? And don't call me that."

"I can't call you Kai?"

"No, not you. You call me Malakai, that's what you say, understood?"

Because you're the only one who has said it that doesn't make me want to hurl or scrub my body until it's raw until my past is washed off me. You don't make me feel slimy when you say it.

I'm not pet.

I'm Malakai.

She nods her head and I start to remind her of the garment I want in my hand, but she begins the process of latching her fingers on the material at her hips. I look down between us, knowing she is watching my face as I witness her slide them down her porcelain thighs.

She is stripping for me, at her work, where anyone could see her. Her obedience makes me weak in the knees.

I'd just planned to take her panties, embarrassing her for pushing me to the point of wanting to touch her.

But the breath was stolen from my lungs when I see the damp spot on the green and white floral thong, I can smell her musky scent leaking from her core and my dick hardens, pushing against my zipper wanting her.

With a hesitant hand, she gives me the panties and I accept them. I roll the material between my fingers, ball them up, and bring them to my nose.

I lock eyes with her as I inhale her scent. Charlotte sinks into the wall as she watches me smell her.

She doesn't smell like fruit or a flower, she smells natural, the way she was made to.

"Malakai, what—"

I step closer to her, not knowing what I was doing either.

I take her panties, stuff them into her pink mouth, and cover it with my palm after. I wanted to keep her quiet, but I also needed a reason not to kiss her.

Me, needing a reason not to kiss someone. Demons must be playing hockey in hell.

I lodge my thigh between her legs, lifting her weightless body up the wall so her feet dangle off the floor. My knee digs into the brick through my jeans, it hurts. I want it to. That's what I get for giving into this. I feel her hot pussy throb on me, and she moans around the fabric in her mouth, making me press into the wall harder.

I knew our height difference would soon prove necessary.

"You're making love to the music, but you were fucking me, weren't you, Moon Eyes?" I rotate my leg just a little and she whimpers, tossing her head back to rest on the brick.

I want her to choke on her arousal like I've been doing every day since she moved in.

She doesn't even shake her head, just falls into a pit of wordless moans. Her hands reach forward to grab my shoulders, but I quickly snatch them with a free hand, shoving them into the brick above her head.

"Grind your pussy all you want on my thigh, but don't touch me," I hiss.

She wants to question it, but when I push harder into her, she's overtaken with too much lust to think about it any further.

"Were you thinking of me stuffing my cock into your mouth up there? Or me punishing your cunt for being so·needy? Look at you, leaking all over my thigh," I whisper as I note her lewd actions.

I remove my hand from her mouth, pulling the fabric out, letting her gasp for fresh air. Her moans become much louder, echoing in my head.

My heart starts pounding harder. My pulse hammering in my ears. I could feel my lungs losing air. I wasn't able to catch my breath. The walls were closing in, it was getting darker, and I was starting to forget where I was.

"Malakai..." she mewls, like a beacon of light at the end of a tunnel her voice pulling me right back in.

I'm not with Yvonne. I'm with Charlotte.

I'm punishing Charlotte for making me want her. I'm fine. I'm okay.

"You made me do this," I say.

She made me want to please her. Want to touch her.

I'd never seen a more erotic sight. Charlotte's fishnet legs clinging to my muscular thigh, riding me as her hair stuck to her forehead from the sweat. How her deprived body seems to be starving for me. I press into her clit harder, wanting her to come.

A hunger to please her overtakes me completely as I move my leg side to side slowly as she rocks up and down. I watch her flushed skin and I can feel her grip tightening on my leg. She's chasing the friction.

The whimpers and moans dissolve into gasps of air, her movements becoming jerky. She loses all rhythm before her body contracts around me. She's been biting her lip trying to stay quiet, now it's all swollen and pink.

I want to know what she tastes like, I need to know.

So I do something I haven't done to any other woman since I was young. I smash my lips into hers, muffling her cries leaving her too convulsive in silence.

My tongue delves into her sultry mouth eating her moans up, swallowing all of them until they are buried in my soul where I am going to keep them.

It doesn't scorch my mouth nor does it taste of battery acid. No, she's sweet, like sugar, like candy. She moves her lips with mine for another lustful moment while her body relaxes.

She was a temple, an eternal empire, and now she's crumbling before me.

"Good God," she sighs.

God. We weren't on good terms, or any terms.

Religion wasn't my thing, but if Charlotte was a religion, I'd worship at her temple every night. I'd pledge my sins to her altar, beg her forgiveness in confession because holding her felt like I had faith in something.

ELEVEN

Kneel to the Throne

CHARLOTTE

J wonder if Cosmopolitan has come out with "How to Not be Awkward Around the Guy You Live with Who Made You Orgasm for the First Time in Your Life WITH HIS THIGH."

I needed someone to help me out of the situation I'd wound up in. Emerson had been my go-to for all of my concerns and problems, but I couldn't talk to him about this for obvious reasons.

So I was stuck, lying in my bed upside down, trying to do homework but not able to focus on anything other than what Malakai was doing. Wondering if he was thinking about what happened a few days ago.

Because after he made me come, the air went from charged to uncomfortable. He didn't say a word to me the entire drive home. Not only was I not wearing panties because mine were in his pocket, but I was flushed and still coming down from my high. He just kept clutching the steering wheel and flexing his jaw like he was angry.

He probably was.

Angry with me for pushing him, angry with himself for falling for it.

He wasn't the kind of man to be pushed to do anything. Malakai, I'm sure, had an awful temper, but it was a controlled kind of anger. He didn't randomly explode. He wasn't the snake striking at everything that came close. He was a panther.

Prowling, lurking, waiting for the perfect moment.

But I'd made him break that control. I had pushed him too far, and watching him unravel was something beautiful.

In a tragic way.

Like when the library of Alexandria came burning down, Julius Caesar must've been in a state of ecstasy when he observed the flames taking down the building that meant little to him. Oh, but Alexander, his greatest treasure was collapsing before him, taking a piece of his soul with it.

There was a glint of wildness in his eyes, a darkness that scared me if I pushed him too far. What could Malakai Petrov do to me?

"Don't touch me."

How could he expect me not to, when all I wanted to do was touch him. But when I'd said his name, he snapped back. The darkness dissolved and he came back from whatever it was that was haunting him.

He came back to me.

I wanted him, but what did he want from me?

Was it the chase he wanted? Was it me? Was it the forbidden aspect of our relationship? Did he want me, for me?

The possibilities of what I and Malakai were doing are endless. My mind is spinning with confusion and unanswered questions. I wanted to know where we stood. I wanted him to touch me again.

I'd never experienced anything like that. I mean, I've had sex. It's enjoyable, never the big O, but enjoyable. That? That was an out-of-body experience. My knees had locked up, my eyes rolled into the back of my head, and I was sure I was possessed.

My door cracks open, and in trots Cebby, Kai's dog. I reach over the side of the bed, petting his smooth black head

"Hey, Cebby," I murmur, the large dog melts in my palm, letting me scratch behind his ears where he has a soft spot. I think he likes me more than Malakai and it makes him angry. When Kai goes to sleep he expects Cerberus to follow him, but normally Cebby sits on the couch with me until I go to bed.

"You want some peanut butter?" I coo as I pet his smooth head. His ears seem to perch up like he understands exactly what I am saying. I smile, nodding my head as I roll out of bed deciding I needed a break anyway.

Cerberus darts out of my room probably already in the kitchen by the time I make it into the hallway. I pass a few rooms on the way out, stopping abruptly when my eyes fall upon something too much for my curious nature to handle.

Malakai's art room is open. Just a sliver, but it's open. That room stays locked, even when he is inside of it.

My fingers zap with electricity, and suddenly the doorknob becomes a magnet for my hand. I just want to peek inside, just a quick look, and then I'll leave.

I do a spin, making sure no one is watching me commit this victimless crime. I know it's wrong, it's an invasion of his privacy, but as Malakai said, my self-control sucks. I just want to see what is going on inside his mind. I want to see what he hides behind the mask, just once.

My fingers push the door open slowly. I cringe when it creaks and decide that I just need to rip the Band-Aid off.

So that's what I do, I open the door quickly and slip inside, pressing my back to the door to shut it. My heart was thumping loudly. Who knew breaking and entering could be such an adrenaline rush?

I take a moment to catch my breath, settling into the smell of paint and turpentine. My eyes aren't sure where to stop at first because there is so much in this room to admire.

Starting with the canvases, big and small, ranging from charcoal sketches of people screaming while they peel their flesh off their faces to designs for new murals I assume from the outlines of different men with large scars on their backs that resemble the ones he has created on the sides of buildings.

There is wickedness harbored in his art, something so painful that I could feel it. He'd left pieces of him in these, so small I don't think he even noticed, but I could feel them.

His emotions.

I could feel each of them brush against my soul in such a distinguished way.

Sadness, melancholy sadness that stayed with you, it felt slippery. Wet, like tears gliding down your face.

Pain, the kind that gets caught in your lungs and lodged in your throat. It was like a carpet burn on my heart.

And unadulterated rage. Anger that only comes from self-loathing. It felt like a tattoo needle, a permanent reminder.

I was so overwhelmed with his feelings, his emotions that he kept behind this locked door that I felt woozy.

My fingers touched the dry pieces of art, looking, inspecting each brushstroke. And that's when I stumbled upon them.

The large canvases nearly my height with different color backgrounds but the same subject.

Women.

There were acrylic paintings of women that were bound by ropes in different positions. It wasn't just hands tied with a rope. No, these women were wrapped with yards of rope. Knots and bows that traveled their bodies.

Some were dangling from the ceiling by their wrists, heads bent, and the fatigue evident even in the painting. Malakai was the kind of artist who made the sweat on their brows seem wet and the skin indents from the rope look soft.

Their bodies were covered in black handprints, his handprints.

I run my finger across the face of one woman who's laying horizontal, suspended in the air with her head thrown back in a mix of pain and pleasure. I was telling myself these were reference photos so I could contain my uncalled-for jealousy.

We weren't anything. Nothing. So what, he made me come and we had one sorta, kinda date. I meant nothing to him, so I had no reason to be jealous when I saw the chains dangling from the ceiling.

Chains that held ropes, that held women Kai brought home, brought into this room.

He must've spent hours, taking his hands across their bodies, tying them up, making them come, fucking them. My stomach flips. Scorching heat runs through me, a love child of jealousy and lust.

I was surrounded by his pleasure, pleasure I wanted to give him, that other women had provided. I want him, even while I'm picturing him with other women, I want him.

I spin around, needing to be away from his room, needing out of here.

I have all intentions of leaving and going straight to my room for the rest of the night, but I realize I'm not alone.

Malakai is standing there, leaning on his work table. One leg kicked up, while his palms hold his weight. I didn't even hear him come in, and now he is standing there, looking at me.

Looking at me like he's seen me come, like he wants to see me naked, drinking me in with his hazel eyes. And I don't know how to breathe properly when he is looking at me like that.

And he's shirtless. As in without a shirt.

The first time I've seen him without one.

My mouth starts to water as I openly gawk at him. Gawking, that wasn't even right, I was stunned. Of course, I knew Kai was good looking and I knew underneath his clothes there was a muscular frame, but seeing his shirtless torso in front of me was different.

I knew people who would kill to look like him, drool worthy.

He had a chiseled chest, his abdominals were sculptured to perfection as his six-pack pops, instantly giving off the impression that he came out of a Calvin Klein shoot. But more than that, the ink that was on his skin flowed effortlessly with every piece of his body. They seemed to move with him, complementing the shape of his abs to the vein on the sides of his neck that were more apparent now.

"Tell me, what do you see, Charlotte?" he says in a steady voice, one that doesn't tell me whether he is angry or calm, all it does is vibrate my core. I was expecting to be yelled at, not quizzed.

"What do you mean?" I ask, hoping my heart doesn't leap out of my throat.

He pushes off the table, coming toward me, stopping to stand directly in front of me and points to the canvases behind me. The ones of the women. Of his women. His muses.

"Tell me, what do you see?"

I don't turn around. I stand my ground staring up at him, gathering some words in my mind.

"Control," I breathe out with all the air in my lungs.

"I see control. If they are bound, they can't hurt you. You are in total control of what they do to you. It's why you use ropes. So you can contain them. I see the beauty in the way you tie them up, you make them into art."

Someone hurt him, badly. Someone had taken his trust in others and spit on it. It's why he prefers being alone, why he's so quiet.

I want to heal his hurt. Soothe his demons.

He stares at me blankly. Nothing passing through his eyes, just standing there staring at me. His right hand raises, he holds it in the air for a second, then he lays it on my cheek so soft, like a butterfly landing on a flower.

"You want me to make you into art, Moon Eyes?" he poses the question so plainly.

I flick my tongue across my bottom lip, wanting to say yes, but I'm choking on the needy lust my body is producing.

I'm achy all over like I was last night performing for him.

"I want to be your muse," I whisper meaning every word.

I wanted him to paint me like those women, to touch me like that.

"My muse? Do you think those women are my muses? You've got it all wrong. My muse comes from pain, a very dark thing living inside of me. Not someone. I break them. They aren't the art, their brokenness is. You want me to make you into my art, Charlotte? Then I'll have to break you." He slides his fingers into my hair holding me there roughly, painfully, but not enough for me to tell him to stop.

"I'm going to tie you up. In very beautiful, sophisticated designs. I'll take my time, making sure each knot accentuates your curves. And I'll make you beg while you're suspended in the air. I will do as

I please. I will tease, exploit, and torment your bound, defenseless body. You will be destroyed when I'm done."

Graphic images of my sweat covered body tethered in ropes while he licks my nipples, or flicks my clit until I'm on the urge of breaking, not orgasming, but shattering into pieces.

"Could you handle that? You couldn't. I won't do that to you. You are whole and untouched. The truth is that I don't want to see you the way I see myself," he pushes.

"So stop pushing me. Stop leaving your panties around, stop fucking sticking your nose into my business. Stop making me want you!" he grunts as he grips the hair at the nape of my neck. My scalp burns.

His threats should scare me. They only succeed in lighting a fire inside of me. In the case of fight or flight.

I'm a fighter.

I place my hands on his chest gingerly, feeling how hot his skin is beneath my fingers.

"Let me show you what I see when I look at you. Let me touch you, and then you can break me, Malakai. You can shatter me, and I'm still going to see you the same." I breathe fire with my words, fire from the passion I feel for him.

I run my hands down to his stomach. My freshly painted blue nails contrast the black ink on his body.

I keep my eyes on him the whole time while I kneel.

I kneel for him, showing him that even though I'm touching him. He's still in control.

My knees dig into the floor, pain biting at me, but I ignore it because this is about him. This is about me showing him that I see him as a beautiful, tortured angel.

My fallen angel.

"What are you doing?" he grunts above me with his jaw clenched and abs contracted.

"Trust me."

I keep my eyes upward even while I'm unbuttoning his pants and pulling the zipper down. Only looking down to tug on them just enough to release his cock, thick and angry. The distinct veins in his girthy shaft that make me lick my lips in anticipation.

He snatches my wrists, holding me, not letting me advance and I stop immediately. I wanted him to trust me, but I'd never push him past what he was comfortable doing.

I move to stand up, but he speaks again.

"Just, just give me a second," he breathes out with his nostrils flaring. He closes his eyes, pinching them tightly. Like he is fighting something inside of him.

"Hey, look at me," I ask, and it takes a moment but he does. Gazing down at me. I wasn't sure what he was fighting, but I knew one thing for certain about Malakai.

He loves my gun-smoke eyes, the ones that I never noticed until him.

"It's me," I say on an exhale, "It's just me."

And he thinks about it, he looks at me, like he's clinging to that fact. A beat passes before he lets me go, nodding his head in approval.

My small hands, tentatively reach out for the base. I roll my hand up, placing my mouth on the tip tasting the tantalizing drop of pre-cum that slides down my throat easily as I take him entirely.

Masculine and strong, that's what he tastes like.

I take my time, worshiping the tip. Letting my tongue swirl and discover the grooves. Just letting him get used to me on him. Allowing him to enjoy this.

"*Trakhni menya*, I knew you had a hot, little mouth," he growls, placing his hands on the back of my head. Since learning Russian I knew those first few words meant *fuck me*.

Usually, someone putting their hands on my head would piss me off, but I wanted him to use me. To use my mouth. To show me how dark he could get.

I engulfed him, licking and rolling my tongue like he was my favorite lollipop. My hand rotates at the base as I descend his shaft, tracing the firm veins popping out with my tongue.

The warmth from his throbbing member heats my mouth. My

saliva gathers along him making it easier for me to slide my lips up and down.

I press my head down to the base, inhaling through my nose, as I hollow my cheeks, sucking hard creating a suction. Kai's grunts above me letting me know that what I'm doing is exactly what he likes. My eyes never moving even though his head is tossed back.

Then his fingers curl into my scalp, clutching me firmly. He pulls his hips back with a groan and strokes forward, hitting the back of my throat creating a wet sound as he crams his cock into my mouth.

He looks down as he continues that process, holding me there as he uses my throat to find pleasure. My eyes start to water the rougher he gets, but I still let him continue his assault on my mouth. I want no part of him to deny that I can handle everything he gives.

I will be selfish, I will take, take, take all he gives.

"Look at you. Look at you taking my cock in your mouth like such a good girl. My good girl."

Good girl makes me shiver with a pleasure I've never experienced before. I wanted to be a good girl, just for him. A good girl who does bad things. Awful, wicked things just with him.

I feel so light-headed at the loss of oxygen. Every time I try to breathe, he thrusts his cock into my throat, stealing all my air, making me have to take short breaths through my nose. It's euphoric.

My body has never felt more alive. His husky voice and deep grunts keep my mouth open and eyes up. It's driving me insane, watching him do this to me.

I was soaked, wetter than I've ever been. My nipples were hard, my legs shaking.

I'm lost in lust, in the sounds his cock makes while making a mess of my mouth, so consumed with all of these emotions and wanting him to finish in my throat that I don't notice when he slows down, only realizing when he pulls out of my mouth with a loud pop.

I blink hazily, while he jerks me up to feet for a split second before I'm lifted off my feet by his stout body. I wrap my legs around his waist, pressing my clothed core against his abdomen, feeling how badly I want him, feeling how desperate I am to have him buried inside of me.

"You didn't let me finish," I mutter.

"I'll go back to destroying that eager throat of yours if you want, but I was thinking I could try something different," he mumbles with his focus on moving me backward.

I reach for the hair tie at the back of his head and pull it loose so that his hair falls down his shoulders, tightening my thighs around his waist.

"That's what I thought."

With a voracious urgency, he pushes me onto the work table.

The sound of brushes and paint cans falling fills the open space. I gasp when I feel something sticky and cold against my neck.

Paint, white paint has spilled onto the table, onto my skin. I look up at Malakai, who has that same wild glint in his eyes as yesterday.

Malakai leans forward, pressing his lips to mine. They are rough where I am smooth, hard where I am soft. It wasn't like one of those close-mouthed kisses like you do when you're in eighth grade, or you're drunk in a bar. It was full, open-mouthed, and full of passion. I melted into his mouth, letting him kiss me. Letting him press his tongue into my mouth and explore.

It's a kiss that makes you feel everything you're supposed to. The sparks, the fireworks, that feeling, it's there and alive.

It's the kiss.

Our kiss.

And when he pulls away an overwhelming feeling hits me in the chest. So strong that I can't keep it to myself.

"I don't want to forget this," I murmur.

I want to hold onto the way his tattoos look right now. How his hair is falling in front of his shoulders in soft waves or the way he is looking at me. I don't want to lose this memory that a picture could never capture.

His eyes soften. The gentleness inside of them hold me.

"I guess I'll have to keep reminding you then."

TWELVE

Masterpiece

KAI

I *don't want to forget this.*
How can one girl be so sweet?
Sweet inside and sweet outside.

Her skin, her lips, her heart, it's all sweet.

I'm dirty, lewd in my soul, and yet when I touch her she isn't tarnished by me. Her milky skin is unscratched as I remove her clothes, article by article exposing another inch of her perfect body. I was touching someone, touching her. Finding tattoos that were hidden. Like the dainty one nestled on her inner thigh that reads:

"Ocean Avenue"

Because she is a sweet, punk loving girl.

People proclaimed they were born in the wrong generation, but it never rang true until her. Charlotte should've been born in the middle of the seventies. The heart and soul of punk rock. With her fishnets and shorts to her beanies with band patches sewn in. She was modern-day punk and I was hard for it.

Hard for her.

"Malakai, *пожалуйста…*" she moans in a needy tone as my lips run across her breast taking her pierced nipple into my mouth and swirling the bud with my tongue, tugging on it with my teeth.

I'm so fucked. Look at her, my smart girl, teaching herself another language. Just for me.

There were no flashbacks, no Yvonne, just her and I. I was euphoric, in a state of ecstasy, and I wasn't even inside of her yet.

She made me feel safe. Unstained.

My dick aches to be inside of her, needing to feel her warmth, to feel how wet she is. Never has the thought of being inside someone made me so greedy, so ferocious. There was this yearning, deep inside of me that needed to be a part of her. To feel what it was like to be with someone like Charlotte.

I've pulled her to the edge of the table, so her naked pussy is grinding up and down my shaft slicking me up with her juices. She's inpatient, messy, unorganized, and everything I claimed to find unattractive.

But looking down, watching her chase the friction, seeing her pink cunt immersing my cock. It makes me groan because there isn't anything hotter than me grabbing her hips and seeing the white imprint of paint I have made on them from the spilled paint can.

"Learning Russian to impress me, Charlotte? You'd do anything I asked wouldn't you, anything to impress me? If I wanted to fuck you in that tight ass you'd let me. If I wanted to shove my dick between your tits and give you a pretty, pearl necklace, you'd let me, wouldn't you?" I ask as I move my hips in sync, making sure to massage the tender bud between her lips that's making her leak all over me.

She nods, sucking her plump bottom lip between her teeth looking so innocent that it makes me weak.

"Yes, yes, yes…" she repeats over and over again.

"Are you going to let me stretch your tiny pussy? It's going to hurt, shoving my thick, fat cock inside of your small walls. I might break you, split you right in half," I murmured, wanting to hear how far she'd be willing to go for me. If she'd let me break her.

All she can manage is a head nod. Her breathless moans match the rhythm of her tensed abdomen while she continues grinding on me like a cat in heat.

I smirk feeling my tip push past her lips and into the narrow passage of her pussy.

She lets out a whine making me thankful for the soundproof walls. After finding her in here, the one place she wasn't allowed, I'd forgotten she was Emerson's sister. She was a girl who had been toeing with a line she should have never messed with.

I was hard before she turned around and kneeled before me.

She let me fuck her face, letting me stay in control. She didn't know about my past, my secrets, my demons, yet she still understood my need to control the situation.

She was imagining what it would be like for me to bind her. Her wide eyes and pouty lips were thinking about what I did to those other women, what they felt like, how hard they came.

Even though I knew she was thinking about it, even though I knew she would have let me tie her up right now, I didn't want to.

I wanted to savor her before I subjected her to the kind of things I did to other women. I wanted to enjoy her body without the ropes, to see her naked flesh and devour everything in my sight.

To see if I could have sex with someone normally.

"*Больше.*"

More.

More she says in a sultry whisper.

Charlotte's body bows into mine as her head tilts back digging into the table. But instead of giving her more as she asked, I stop abruptly. My dick not even halfway inside of her. I need to stop. There are images trying to push their way into my head, and I needed something to ground me before I ruin this moment.

"Look at me, Moon Eyes. I want to see those eyes when I ruin you," I demand.

This was a kink I'd recently developed. One I'm sure only applied to her. I liked looking at her. I liked it when she looked at me.

She saw things in my eyes others haven't seen in me in years. They kept me grounded.

A fallen angel that fell, just for her.

She follows what I say, opening her eyes, and looking right at me.

I let out a moan, clearly enjoying the way her tight walls embrace me. I hold tight to her hips, as I continue to push inside of her inch by inch until I'm buried within her.

Charlotte becomes a whimpering mess. The few drops of sweat gather on her forehead as she works hard to accommodate my size. My eyes shift down focusing on the way my length looks spearing into her dripping wetness.

"That pussy looks so good with my cock shoved inside of it, don't you think?" I ask, holding her hip with one hand and placing my other one on the side of her neck to hold it gently.

I lean into her body, placing my lips to hers, swallowing the yes on her tongue. The urge to kiss someone had never hit me the way it did with her.

She is so tiny in my grasp, jiggling with every deep thrust which only helps in spurring my movements. I began pounding into her, faster and faster. My muscles are on fire as I piston my hips into her.

"I'm so full, you're everywhere," she whines.

"Good, I want you to be full of me, Charlotte. Too much of me. Overflowing with me."

I hold her in place by her neck, moving my hand from her hip to her clit eagerly pushing it in short, tight circles wanting to give her the blissful feeling she is seeking.

"Your cock feels so good, you feel so good." She squeezes my dick with her walls, pulsing around me. While her hands wrap around my forearm, digging into my skin and clinging to my body.

No woman ever dirty talked to me the way she was. My girl had a filthy little mouth, one that was twisting me into knots.

"Fuck…" I grunt, with my cock all the way inside of her, her tunnel feeling impossibly tight. The only thing that was left was for me to abandon it, pulling my hips back before slamming my cock home into her again.

I start to thrust with abandon again, stroke after stroke as my raw cock rails into her.

"Oh God, I'm about to—"

"I know, baby, I know, *детка*," I coo, cradling her face with my free hand.

She cries out wanting to shut her eyes, but she obeys my order by keeping them on me. They stay locked to mine as those celestial gems shatter in pleasure. She becomes a vise of warmth as her pussy spasms around me. I know she is coming. I can feel her, but I continue my assault on her clit, wanting her to give me everything she has.

She screams while she tries to push my hand away, attempting to run away from the pleasure I am giving her. That feeling of wanting to explode right there, an intense climax she's afraid of.

"No, you stay right fucking there and take it, Charlotte," I growl, tightening my grip on her face, holding her in place and not letting her run away from this orgasm.

And because Charlotte is such a good girl, she takes it.

Her body is convulsing in sporadic shakes as her core gushes all over my cock and hand. The glistening juices that spill from her send me over the edge.

"Goddamn it, that's hot," I grunt as my abdominal muscles tighten, and I feel my release creeping up on the back of my heels.

I pull out of her soaking walls and finish myself off onto her stomach. Coming with a moan as thick, hot streams of my seed shoots onto her skin. My final brush stroke on what is my greatest work of art.

I look at the mess I have made on her tattooed stomach. The paint, sweat, and come that decorate her porcelain skin. She's breathing heavy, her body still trembling from her release.

I'd been working with art since I was a teenager. I'd seen a lot, painted a lot of naked women, but nothing compared to her. To this.

The random handprints on her body, her blue hair sprawled out beneath her, the pink flush on her cheeks, her eyes. I don't realize I'm staring until she says something.

"What are you looking at?" she asks.

So, I answer her, truthfully.

"You wanted me to make you into art, right?"

She nods, tiredly. I lean forward, pressing my lips to her forehead, sighing.

"You were already a work of art, Charlotte. But now, you're my masterpiece."

THIRTEEN

Remember this

CHARLOTTE

"As soon as I'm done here, I'll be at the game. I'll make it before the second period."

I put my car into park, opening the door, and starting my walk to the front doors of the senior living community.

"You sure you're coming? Because you've been flaking on me lately," Emerson responds, making my stomach sink.

"I missed one movie night. You're the one who's never home. Half the time I never know where you are."

"Hockey, Charlie. I've just been practicing a lot."

That's a lie.

I want to be optimistic. I want to believe that he's not back on drugs and he is just working hard, but he isn't.

A few days after Malakai and I had sex, they went on the road for a few away games, but when they came back, I'd seen Kai every day for the past month when he wasn't at practice or playing. Yet, Emerson was nowhere to be seen.

He could be seeing someone, but I doubt it because the red tint is starting to make an appearance in his eyes again.

I'm torn.

Torn between Malakai and Emerson.

109

I feel like the time for me to choose between someone who makes me happy, and my family is dawning. I'm either going to have to break things off with Kai or convince him to tell my brother about us.

Juggling both separately is too hard. I feel in a constant state of war. Being with Malakai, but worrying about Emerson. Keeping an eye on Emerson, but missing Kai.

"Maybe we can grab dinner after your game tonight?"

"That sounds good. I'll see you tonight, love you, Charlie."

"Love you too, Em."

And then I'm left with dead silence on the other end as I stroll into the facility. It smells like baby powder and some type of festive candle. Peppermint, reminding me of Christmas at my childhood home.

I used to love the holidays, decorating, making gingerbread houses, cooking thanksgiving dinner, but now it all seemed pointless.

It felt like I was making memories just to forget them.

Emerson and I didn't celebrate Thanksgiving this year, and I worked on Halloween. The happiest time of the year was becoming gloomier with each passing day.

I check in with the front desk and walk toward my mother's private room at the back of the facility. They try to make it as homey as possible, but it's a joke. There is nothing homey about losing a loved one. Walking into the tiny room seeing her lying in the bed attached to a feeding tube because she's lost motor function in her mouth and won't eat was something I was never prepared for.

The pneumonia has taken a toll on her body, while the treatments have stopped for the disease, it speeds up the Alzheimer's. She was just a body with a vacant stare now, she seldom made noise. It was a shell.

This condition was so grim. It not only took its victim's life, but it took their memory. They say you can't take earthly possessions when you die, so it's best to make experiences cause that's all you can take.

Alzheimer's patients don't even get that.

This scares me because I don't want my mom to die with nothing. I want her to treasure that she was an amazing mother, an astonishing teacher, a friend, a wife.

I fight the tears, wanting to get through this visit without breaking down.

"Hey, Mom."

She doesn't move her head or eyes, still gazing straight ahead, as if nothing was said. Before the pneumonia, she would look at people when they talked to her, but she didn't comprehend what they were saying.

It used to make me laugh because she replied with one of three things always.

"That's good, sweet pea."

"Oh how funny!"

"Love you!"

No matter the context of the conversation, it was one of those. An English teacher who had been stripped of nothing but three sentences. I hated how painful the world could be.

"I'm sorry I haven't been to visit, it's just hard seeing you like this, ya know? It's hard because I cherish who you were and I want to remember that. The one who decorated the house in thousands of Christmas lights and yelled at Emerson for breaking the bulbs or playing hockey in the driveway. I don't want to remember you this way, Mom," I tell her honestly, wiping the tears that fall down my face.

"I brought you some pictures of Em. He's still a dork," I chuckle, pulling out pictures from my bag.

I sift through them, holding them in front of her face.

"I printed off a few articles about him too. I'll leave them here for you. He is doing good, Mom. I think he misses you more than he likes to admit, but that's Em, right? Always holding his problems in."

I'm talking to myself, but it feels good to get it off my chest. To talk to someone, which is why I came here. I needed someone to talk to.

I can't talk to Emerson about this, and I don't have friends. Not real friends who would give me advice or help me through this. I had surface friends.

So that left my mother. She couldn't reply, but I could imagine she was.

"I met a guy."

I believe she would squeal, clap her hands, and hug me. Tell me she knew I'd find someone one day. Someone who would love me, blue hair and all.

"His name is Malakai, and I brought some pictures of him too." I smile sorrowfully, pulling the pictures out of my bag and holding them in front of her face. The one that still hasn't moved, I think she's blinked twice.

"I think you would like him, Mom. I saw him reading the other day, John Keats." I laugh. "I know you prefer Tennyson, but I think you'd make an exception for him. Do you remember when you used to read to me?" I showed her a Polaroid of Kai who was sitting on the couch with a book in his hands.

He'd ignored me the first few days after having sex. Took time away in his room, but he'd started to come out more. Watching movies with me, spending time with me.

I'd taken all these without his permission, afraid it would spook him.

I was getting to know him, other sides of him. I was learning that he thought of himself as empty when he was a museum full of things.

From his ability to cook to art, his intelligence, and knowledge of the world. Even if he got angry that I beat him in Jeopardy, being around him still made me happy. He made small things special.

And he loved watching me perform.

He didn't think I noticed but I did. I saw him watching me, pausing to listen. It was the perfect excuse to practice for my audition coming up.

I felt like a world-touring violinist when he watched me. He looked at me like there was something worth looking at.

"And he's an artist. He is so talented, everything he does is stunning. From murals to stick figures, they could hang next to Picasso." My trembling hands switch to another image, one of Kai with his back to me and his scars on display.

There are so many long, nasty scars on his back. The black ink from his tattoo, the tattoo of two large black wings covers them up, but you can still see the raised skin.

The tattoo work is throttling. The feathers look soft like at any moment they are going to extend from his back and he is going to soar. Something in his past had made him feel unworthy, but he'd kept his wings.

The angel who was curious about what was down below and tumbled below the clouds.

The guardian who wanted to protect the ones that roamed beneath.

He hadn't fallen from grace because he was evil, he fell to prevent it.

I continue showing Mom the pictures of him making me Russian dumplings, another of him wrestling with Emerson, his painting, and my favorite is of him looking right at me. His hair is down in his face, just how I like and he is glaring.

Angry because I'm taking his picture, but the smirk that tugs at his lips tells me he's being playful.

"He makes me happy and he doesn't even know it," I say.

I can hear Mom saying, *So what's the problem, sweet pea?*

So I keep talking like she is listening.

"But, he's hiding something, keeping something from me, Mom. And I want to know everything, you know me. I have to know everything. I want to meet his friends, to figure out if he snores at night, know where he stands, know what it's like to be loved by him."

I slam my hand in front of my mouth like I just spilled a secret that wasn't ever supposed to be told.

I'd never said those words before. Not to anyone other than Em and Mom. I'd never said those words to or about anyone.

I love him.

I'm not shocked. I knew when I met him that I was going to love him.

I knew deep down in my heart I'd found someone special in that hooded graffiti artist with hazel eyes. I didn't know if he'd be my forever, but he was something.

It's a feeling you get when you meet people, the one where you know deep in your gut they are going to mean something to you. They are going to be your Edward Lewis to your Vivian Ward. Like when Noah first saw Allie at the carnival?

I knew when Kai saved me from nearly dying that he was going to be something spectacular.

"Mom, I'm in love," I say with a laugh, a few tears falling as I look at her and she's still staring straight ahead.

Maybe she's not in there anymore, and I'm just talking to a hollow person, but it's comforting to know that she may be, and she knows her little girl is in love and happy.

FOURTEEN

Crossing the Line

KAI

"After the challenge that New York gave you in this game, what do you think your team needs to do to prevent close calls like this one?"

I run my fingers through my wet hair wanting to be anywhere else but in this room. I had almost made it out of the locker room, but the vultures spotted me and now I was stuck answering questions.

"I think we just have to keep it simple, capitalize on our chances, and create some opportunities. Like I said earlier, just getting pucks deep and getting them out," I reply with some of the most cliché hockey talk because I want out of here as fast as possible.

"Some are saying that call at the end wasn't right. Saying the puck went past the goal line, how do you feel about that?"

There is always some douchebag that tries to get you riled up with stupid questions.

"What do you think?" I pose, looking down at him and his microphone that is shoved a little too close to my face.

"I saw the replay, you saw it, the refs saw it. It was on the jumbotron. It stayed on our side, if people want to speculate then that's fine, but the game is over and on record. We won, that's all that matters to me. Thanks guys," I finished slinging my bag over my head and moving to the exit so I could leave and get home.

There is something pleasurable about the pressure my position holds. An adrenaline rush from the responsibilities on my shoulders. People don't understand it, watching my job on TV? It seems easy. All I have to do is prevent the puck from entering the net.

People don't understand the weight that comes from being a goaltender. Do people notice when Frenchie's defense gap is too big? Hardly. Does anyone see Nico not back checking? Possibly, but I doubt it. However, everyone notices my mistake.

Because when I fuck up? There is a loud buzzer that alerts the entire arena that I messed up. My mistakes are tallied at the end of the game. The score tells everyone how I did.

Not everyone can be a goalie and that's why I liked the position. It takes a unique person to put on equipment and stand in front of hockey pucks coming straight at you at 100 miles per hour. I have less than a second to react, to protect the goal.

The other guys took their time getting ready, but it took me countless hours over my career to figure out the way I liked my pads strapped and my pants tied. Whether or not to tuck my chest protector or leave it hanging out. I'd finally found my favorite stick height, weight, and curve. There were so many little aspects that went into making me the athlete I am.

I liked being in the shadows, sitting behind my mask. I didn't want to be the star of the show like Nico.

"Dadadada, this is SportsCenter! I'm here with Malakai Petrov, tell me, how does it feel to commit larceny on one of the best forwards in the league?" Nico jokes, holding a fake microphone to my mouth, as we walk out of the locker room, mimicking the music introduction to ESPN. An ongoing joke between athletes that when you do something great in a game, your teammates make the ESPN noise meaning you'll probably be featured on it later.

"Don't you have a woman to get to?" I say chuckling.

"I do, she's waiting for me in the tunnel. Is purple panties waiting for you?" He elbows me in the ribs and I roll my eyes. He still hasn't let that shit go.

The game against New York was left tied at the end of three regular timed periods, and after going into overtime with still no one scoring, it was left to a shootout.

A shootout is when three skaters take alternating turns shooting penalty shots against the opposing goaltender.

In layman's terms, it had come down to me to make sure we pulled this win out.

Emerson played a hell of a game tonight, his defense had been some of the best I'd seen from anyone in a long time, but New York was on our heels the entire game. They were a solid well-rounded team and most sports analysts had predicted them to make a run for the cup.

Nico had been the only man to score, leaving us up one. All I had to do was block one more shot.

Those moments are my favorite part. I was in control of the outcome completely and there was nothing I loved more than control. I'd blocked the first two shots easily, but stayed humble.

Getting angry when a shot goes in doesn't help me. I have to stay levelheaded, focused on the next shot because I'm only as good as my last save. I have realized over the years that I'm going to make mistakes, I can't save every puck. But I have to do everything I can to try to.

It's my job to play with a consistent intense calmness the entire game.

The forward had been standing down the ice, needing to score in order to extend the shootout. He needed it for his team, for his fans, for himself. I could see how he squeezed his stick, trying to breathe and steady his heart rate.

I was focused on the puck, focused on him. During normal game play my mind would be racing with scenarios of what could happen, what I needed to prepare my body to do while there was a play already developing in front of me.

He had skated forward, scooping the puck with his blade as he passed center ice, heading toward me, and that was when the crowd began to rumble. I blocked them out, the shouts, the screams were nothing but muffled noise.

My glove was up and open. My stick between my legs protecting the five-hole, and my feet were just wide enough to help me move around the net. The forward had skated left, quickly pushing the puck ahead of him, pulling his stick back for a slapshot at the top of the face-off circle.

But I'd seen how far the puck was from him and knew it was a fake. An attempt to get me to fold. So I had withheld from reacting and he had to form a new game plan.

He'd been dancing, pulling the puck from his back hand to his forehand, back and forth trying to get me to give my position, to break one direction or the other, to give him an opening.

My eyes had been too focused on the puck and not his movements, and he succeeded on pulling me right. I had dropped to my knees thinking he was taking the shot, but he lagged to the left.

I thought it was over then. I gave it my last shot, having rolled my body and stuck my glove behind my back in hopes to block the puck from going in.

I wasn't even sure I'd caught it until the boys rushed the ice congratulating me.

"Nico, I think Riggs would be a little upset if she heard you talking about another girl's panties, don't you?" I motion toward the blonde waiting at the bottom of the tunnel waiting for him.

Nico shoves my shoulder jokingly and I laugh, looking up again but this time I catch a glimpse of bright blue hair.

I'd heard them talking about her coming to the game, and I knew she was here for him, but for a split second I thought,

So this is what she would look like waiting for me after games.

Soft curls, an oversized jersey that she tucked into a pair of black ripped skinny jeans with a beanie looking so out of place in this hockey arena.

What I was doing was wrong, stupid, and reckless.

Sleeping with a teammate's sister, wait I forgot to mention, an emotional imbalanced teammate's sister, is asking for trouble.

And I should have no problem looking the other direction. I could get another woman, any other woman. Someone less complicated, someone who doesn't need me to open the pickle jar.

Someone who doesn't wear mismatched socks and leave sticky notes on the bathroom mirror. Anyone else in the world, and yet I couldn't tell her no.

I couldn't quit Charlotte.

I hadn't had sex with her again, even though I craved it. I wanted to so badly, but I couldn't. I tried distancing myself again, but she just kept showing up.

She was like smoking but worse.

I'd never enjoyed smoking in the first place. It was something to do with my hands, something to numb my mind when I was going through hell.

I vowed to leave my past, to leave Yvonne in Russia. I didn't tell anyone about it, not Nina, not Bishop, Nico, none of them. I've never told anyone what happened to me except the cigarettes.

Charlotte was making me think I could tell her things; that she would understand. But I knew better, when I told her, she'd look at me and see how filthy I am. She'd be disgusted.

Being self-aware, I knew I would struggle with PTSD. I had been sexually abused most of my childhood. I think it would be odd if I didn't have some sort of problem in adulthood.

So when the memories would get too much, when they started to eat at me, and I looked down at my skin and saw all the dirt Yvonne had left, I smoked.

Then I found art and I quit smoking cold turkey.

Art and smoking was a spiritual cleansing. It was a shower that briefly washed away the sins from my skin, the pain from deep inside of my chest.

And right before I met Charlotte, I was losing grip on art, because the truth was I was still ashamed of what I'd been through. I held my life together seamlessly, but underneath the mask, I was just a man trying to forget the scars he carried on his back.

"Who is the chick with blue hair?" Nico jolts me out of my thoughts and I clear my throat.

"Emerson's twin, Charlotte."

"Well isn't that unfortunate," he replies.

I bring my eyebrows together. "Unfortunate?"

He nods, pulling his bag higher on his shoulder. "Yeah, because you're looking at her like she isn't Emerson's sister. If I were you, big man, I would tell him before he finds out."

I never thought I would see the day that Nico Jett would be giving me advice.

I once had to carry him out of a bar after he bought an entire bottle of Patron for himself. That's also the same night he threw up on my shoes. And he is giving me advice on women?

Yeah, my life has gone to shit.

Nico leaves my side to try to make a baby with Riggs, while Emerson jogs past me to Charlotte who is still staring at her cell phone because she is nervous. This place isn't her crowd, and it's making her uncomfortable.

But once Emerson pokes her sides, she smiles, hugging him. I take my time walking toward them, giving them space to have their family bonding. When she spots me a wide smile breaks out on her face, which makes my stomach drop.

Butterflies.

I, a grown-ass man, am getting butterflies.

"What's up, Superstar? I didn't think someone as big as you could move like that." She smirks.

"I'm just full of surprises," I reply, letting the smile tugging at my lips appear.

Maybe Emerson isn't the only player she came to watch.

Emerson's phone starts ringing and instead of answering it, he takes one look at the screen and shoves it into his pocket, like it's on fire.

"Yeah, no kidding," he laughs nervously. "Hey, did you know he's that graffiti artist you've been obsessed with since like high school?" he blurts out, scratching the back of his neck.

"Emerson!" Charlotte squeals.

I look at him attentively, clenching my jaw.

"Can you keep your voice down?" I say with irritation riddling my voice. I was an anonymous artist, and I wanted to stay that way.

"Come on, man. It's just Charlie. I've kept that secret in for like a year. I had to tell someone. Plus, you have something to talk about tonight. I have to stop somewhere on the way home, so you guys go ahead," he instructs, smiling a little too wide. Like it's forced.

I open my mouth to ask where he is going, but she beats me to it.

"You told me we could grab a late dinner after the game. Where are you even going?"

He sighs, rubbing his face with his hands like he's uneasy. Except I know what it is, that's a drug addict wanting their next fix.

He's craving.

"We still can! I'll only be twenty minutes. I swear, Char," he lies straight through his teeth, right to her face.

Rage burns in my stomach, when I see the look of acceptance and defeat settle on her face. She doesn't want to argue with him here, but I do.

"Why don't I stop and get whatever it is you need, so you can head home with her."

His shaky eyes snap to me, and I give him a fake smile so he knows I'm onto him.

"No, man, I got it. I won't be long." He tries shaking me off with another bullshit lie. But I keep pushing him.

"It's cool, let me do it—"

"Dude, get the fuck off my back! I can do it. Just take her home," he yells, throwing his hands in front of him to extend his point.

Charlotte steps toward him, trying to reach out for him but he pushes her off. "I'll be home later, Charlotte."

I grab her by the waist pulling her behind me, so that I'm face to face with Emerson.

"Lay your hands on her again. I dare you," I fume.

He gives me a crooked grin. The coke flowing through his veins giving him a god complex that thinks he won't lose to me in a fight.

"You're gonna tell me how I should and shouldn't touch women? A little hypocritical for a guy who gets his rocks off by hurting them," he snarks.

One drunken night, he stumbled into my old apartment and

went into the wrong room. He saw one painting in my workroom, one of the women tied up and he thinks I'm so sort of sadist.

I suck my teeth, smiling threateningly, nodding my head up and down.

"You think you're a tough guy, don't you? You're a fucking druggie, who is losing the only people he has left."

I stare into his green eyes seeing my words hurt him and it makes me regret saying them. But not enough to take them back.

"Guys, people are watching," Charlotte says, tugging on my arm.

I step back from him, giving him space,

"Em, please—"

But he's already leaving, shrugging his leather jacket onto his shoulders, not bothering to turn around. I look down at her and there is a profound sadness in her eyes that makes me so furious at him I could murder him.

I know the feeling she has in her heart when the empty promises of an addict become hard truths. When you realize they never were getting better, they just got better at sneaking it.

FIFTEEN

For you, I would

KAI

"*H*ey oh, listen what I say, oh."

My eyes pop open, expecting to be dead and at a Red Hot Chili Peppers concert in hell, but I'm greeted with the sight of my living room.

My neck aches when I sit up and when I tilt it back and forth it pops like fireworks. I rub my eyes looking down at my shirtless torso and grey sweatpants confused as to why I woke up on my couch.

"When it's killing me, when will I really see." A voice is coming from outside of my house harmonized with the barking of my dog, and that's when I realize that I not only fell asleep on the couch, I fell asleep with Charlotte.

I smack myself on the forehead, over and over again.

"Stupid, stupid, fucking idiot," I grumble.

I'm angry, not because I regret it, but because I don't want to hurt her. She is going to get attached to me, and then I'm going to have to break her heart.

I don't want that.

Charlotte had been quiet the entire drive home, the silence was so loud I needed to play music. I know what it's like to feel the way she does, and I also know that if people want to talk about something, they will.

123

Pushing someone only irritates them.

When she went upstairs I thought she was staying up there, so I made myself a drink and got comfortable on the couch preparing myself to wait up for Emerson.

He wasn't coming home anytime soon, we both knew that.

But surprisingly she came back down the steps, holding a pillow and wearing pajamas. Calmly she put in a movie and sat next to me on the couch.

I looked over at her and felt like shit.

This is why I don't get attached to people. Because of what could happen to them once I allowed myself to care.

What if she left?

What if she hurt me?

What if she died?

To me for the longest time, it was better to be alone than to worry about what-ifs that came with caring about people.

But there is nothing that feels quite like Charlotte.

For the first time when I touched someone, it didn't feel wrong. I didn't see the dirt leftover on their skin from my foul spirit.

I left black paint prints on the other women, so it would show what happens when I'm allowed to touch pure things.

But that didn't happen with her.

Yvonne had labeled me, scarred me, burned into me that all I would be was a person who infected other people. She'd rubbed her impurity onto me before I even knew what that meant.

She'd forced me to defile someone else after she'd broken me. She was the worst kind of evil. The kind that makes it feel like it's your fault.

Do you know what it's like to be a child at an altar begging God to cleanse you? Apologizing for the rottenness and the bad you'd done when you were the victim?

Because I do.

But I'd never felt forgiven until I touched her and she remained flawless, unstained, untainted.

Robotically she tilts her body onto the couch, laying her head on her pillow and stretching her feet toward me. What do I do here? What should I do? How do I make this better?

I do exactly what I needed as a kid.

I decide to hold her.

I grab her waist, scooting her forward, giving me enough room to slip behind her. I lay my head on the pillow, wrapping an arm around her waist and I pull her into my chest.

Cuddling.

Can't say I'd ever saw myself participating in this.

When I hear the first sniffle, that's when I know she's crying. A gnawing in my chest starts, I'm hurting for this small thing in my arms. She rotates so that she is facing me, and she buries her face into me.

I cover her with both of my arms, creating a protective shell for her to find sanctuary in.

"It's okay, Moon Eyes, you can disappear here for a little while."

She doesn't answer me, only vibrates more with the heavy tears she is leaking. I can feel them on my naked chest and they feel like acid melting straight through my rough exterior.

Soon, her breathing evens out, her chest rises and falls promptly, and I know she's starting to fall asleep.

I'll just lay here until she is sleeping deeply, then I'll get up. That's what I tell myself as my eyes start to grow heavy, sandbags holding them down, and the smell of peppermint starting to soothe me to sleep.

I stand up from my spot and start following her voice. I follow it straight out the front door where I find her in the yard, spinning in circles while snow falls from the sky. Cerberus is running around her, yapping at the falling ice, and she laughs as she tries to sing.

I was feeling this tight pressure in my chest, something that made me move back inside the house and search for her purse. It was probably wrong going through it, but in the long run, she'd thank me. I pull the Polaroid camera out that she's always waving in my face and jog back outside.

I lean on the banister pointing the lens toward her, waiting for the perfect moment to snap the picture.

Black and white striped long sleeve shirt underneath a huge Nirvana t-shirt that looks like it might fit me. Tight combat boots, skinny jeans that look thrifted.

Muffed headphones that are too big on her small head.

Pale, curvy, blue among all the white in the snow.

I click the button, waiting for the picture to develop just in time for her notice that I'm standing there. Her opaque skin is tinted pink from the cold, and her eyes are brighter than I've ever seen them.

"What are you doing with my camera?" she asks out of breath.

I lift the picture, wiggling it a little, before shoving it into the pocket of my sweats.

"Maybe I want to remember a few things too."

I can't tell if it's from being cold or embarrassment, but her cheeks turn even pinker. It makes me laugh. She kneels, petting Cerberus who purrs into her touch like a cat.

We are both becoming softies, pal.

Her head tilts back letting the frozen rain touch her face freely, and she looks so peaceful. Like an angel.

I'm the dark one, the one who fell to earth for selfish reasons, the one damned to live life with scars on my back reminding me forever that I fell from grace.

But I think they gave my wings to Charlotte.

It's everything I represent in my art. Fallen angels whose wings are given to ones who can use them.

Falling was worth it if it meant she could fly.

"Happy?" I ask.

"Euphoric," she says on an exhale.

"When I was young, my mom, Emerson, and I would dance in the first snowfall. Every year, that would be the day we would start decorating for Christmas. It didn't matter when it was. Em hated it." She giggles about the memory.

I never had a memory like that growing up. Only once my mom came home with a tattered book, it was Pushkin, and it was the only thing she ever gave me.

Besides the trauma, of course, that was the gift that just keeps giving. Like chlamydia. Which she also had, I'm sure.

"I guess we need to go buy Christmas decorations then, huh?" I offer.

Shock registers, then she squints her eyes like she thinks I'm tricking her. I don't blame her, I feel like I'm playing a practical joke on myself.

"The prince of darkness is going to let me decorate his house?" she says with a weary voice.

Oh, I'm going to have a say in it, she is not putting pink or purple lights anywhere, but we will cross that bridge when we get to Ikea.

"Is it going to keep you happy, like this?"

Is it going to distract you from the fact your mom is dying and your brother is killing himself with drugs?

She watches me for a moment, just standing there staring at me. I'd give anything to read her mind.

Slowly, she nods her head up and down signaling a yes as she stands up, moving up the steps toward me.

My skin is already ice cold when she lays her dainty hands on my chest, staring up at me like I just gave her the world.

I flinch a little, pulling back from her touch.

"Then yes, I'm going to let you decorate the house," I say.

"Where is Emerson, do you want him to come?" I ask.

"Passed out, probably. He got home at sunrise. You slept through our argument, thankfully. I'll let him sleep." She tucks a piece of hair behind her ear like them fighting is embarrassing.

"And let me guess, he smelled like a trap?"

"Yeah." She mumbles, "Can I hug you, please?"

She needed me, needed me to be someone different than cold Malakai. The Malakai who played Jeopardy with her and let her take pictures of him when she thought he wasn't paying attention.

The Malakai only she got.

I nod, and she steps into my space, dropping her forehead to my naked chest, hiding her face. I wrap my arms around her, pulling her closer.

A trap was short for a trap house, where drunks and druggies hang out. They swapped products, got fucked up beyond recognition, and most of them crashed on the dirty floors.

It carries a stench, like stale cigarettes, vinegar, and gasoline. This sounds like an odd combination until you've smelled cocaine residue on someone's skin and walked by a used heroin needle.

I place my hands on the sides of her face, tilting her eyes up at me.

"I won't if you tell me not to, but I'm going to tell the general manager of Fury. I'd rather him lose his career than his life, Charlotte."

I rub my thumbs on her cheeks, trying to comfort her.

"Let me talk to him first? Just one last time and then you can. I'm afraid what will happen when we take away hockey. I don't know what he will do with himself."

"He'll have us. He has friends, ones that will be there. He has you, he has you, Charlotte." I emphasize.

"If I had to guess you're the only reason he's trying to fight his addiction, without you? He'd be too far gone," I say, hoping my honesty doesn't hurt her too badly.

Instead of replying, she stretches on her tiptoes as far as she can before I need to bend to meet her. I have a choice, I could step back and walk inside, lock myself in my room while she decorates, or I could kiss her.

I place my hands on the sides of her face, pulling her into me, our lips meeting in the middle.

SIXTEEN

When the World went Dark

CHARLOTTE

*C*hristmas.
The most wonderful time of year.

It's the time when families come together, sit and talk about how great it is to be here. Or in my case, you finish decorating an entire living room, put up a tree, while Malakai tries to untangle the Christmas lights.

Emerson left earlier, saying he wouldn't be home till late even after I begged him to stay and decorate. I even bribed him with sugar cookies, but it wasn't enough.

I'd bought an ungodly amount of things at the store because Kai had zero, I mean zero decorations. We'd decided on going with the Fury colors, black, white and red. So we got a black tree with red bulbs and white lights.

I tried matching everything else in the house to that color scheme and surprisingly it gave off the perfect vibe. He just doesn't know about the strategic candle warmers I have hidden from him that are filling the house with wonderful holiday scents.

I'd just made peppermint tea and sat on the couch, watching him. The frown on his brow told me he was stressed, but his pose remained poised. A bomb could go off in the next room and I'm positive he would remain stoic.

What he is, what is distracting about him, comes from his spirit; it makes me want to feel his lips on mine, to hear his heartbeat beneath my ear in bed, to know what it sounds like when he says I love you.

The demeanor of a demon and the soul of an angel.

"Done," he grunts, pulling the last knot from the cord. I set my tea down, grabbing the plug and finding an outlet quickly to make sure all the bulbs work. I turn to see the hardwood floor lit up with white.

They look like stars on the floor, like the heavens fell in Kai's living room.

"Here, do me a favor," I say, jogging to my purse and grabbing my camera, handing it to him.

"I'm gonna lay in the lights and you take a picture of it," I insist. I'd always thought these pictures were so cool and never had a chance to get any myself, so this seemed like the perfect opportunity.

I sit on the floor, careful not to crush the bulbs, and start to drape them over me hoping they look somewhat organized. Malakai stands above me, watching with his aloof stare that makes me wonder what he's thinking.

"You can fix them if they don't look right," I offer, trying to fix them myself, but I'm sure they look stupid.

"Do you trust me, Charlotte?" he asks above me.

I knit my eyebrows, nodding up and down slowly.

"Say it."

"I trust you, Malakai."

From standoffish to obscene his gaze shifts. Like he removed one mask and put on another.

With a tremendous amount of aggression, lust, and even a touch of anger, he pulls me up by underneath my arms and has me stand in front of him. I swallow the nerves in my throat, curious as to what he is going to do next.

Nonchalantly he starts to remove my clothes. I recoil from his touch when his icy fingers skim my ribs as he takes my shirt off. He looks down at me with concern, pulling away a little.

"No, no, your hands were just cold," I reassure him that I want this, that I trust him, whatever it is he wants to do.

The rest of my clothes fall at the touch of his palms until I'm completely naked. He'd seen me naked before, and prior to him, I'd never given a fuck what people thought about how I looked.

Until I was standing here with him examining me. Walking around me in circles, eyeing me up and down. I think about all the women in the paintings, how their bodies looked. No extra skin, no scars, tan. They were long-legged models, and I was feeling insecure.

I'd accepted the fact I had a stomach, that no matter what I ate or how much I worked out it was still going to stay there. My thighs were never going to have a gap, and I am the color of a ghost.

"Are you trying to count my stretch marks?" I try to joke, hoping if I laugh first it won't be as bad.

"Just figuring out how it's possible for one person to be so perfect," he says it like it's the most obvious statement in the room. My insecurities dissolve, and in its place a sexual goddess who wants to be touched.

But Malakai isn't rushing. He's working, he's taking his time. He picks up the string lights, dragging his hands across them, and once he figures out what he wants to do, he binds me.

There is something extremely erotic about this process.

As his fingers and hands work to wrap me delicately in lights, he grazes over my skin, shocking me with lust each time. The warmth of the bulbs heat my skin. He wraps them over my shoulders and underneath my breasts making a design of Christmas lights on my upper body. It makes a Y down the valley of my chest, leaving my pierced nipples and breasts exposed with lights beneath and above. It compresses them.

A breathy moan escapes when he works lower. He's so focused, so attentive. His skilled fingers work quickly wrapping my lower half in a design that squeezes my inner thigh tightly. It reminds me of a harness that people use for rock climbing.

He's binding my body and tethering my heart.

"Fuck," I groan as he pulls tighter on the one closest to my crotch, it's a tease. He is teasing me. Watching me, tying me up, touching me, but not giving me what I want.

My lust was unquenchable by the time he was finished.

I can sense his mood shift from artist to I want to shove my cock into all of your holes. The way he grabs me and lays me onto the floor, even though I have full control of my hands. His power stance above me has my legs tilting open, inviting him between my hips needing something, needing him.

Casually, he drops one knee between my legs, as his large hands pry my hips open causing the lights to contract around me. I revel the pain of it. The burn, the sting, being with him.

"Malakai, please do something," I wiggle, panting with desire.

He leans down to me, placing both of his hands flat on the ground beside my head, placing a chaste kiss on my lips.

"Patience is a virtue, Charlotte," he mumbles, biting my bottom lip, before dipping his hips between mine. The fabric of his jeans rubbing against my clit. I instantly reach up, gripping his shoulders trying to push myself into him more.

A gasp leaves my lips as his hand grasps my breast, kneading it in his palm. The metal barbells bite into my skin.

"Don't stop doing that," I breathe

He places another kiss to my lips, "You like that, don't you?" he muses, smirking over my mouth.

"You like the pain." He continues squeezing hard, making my body jerk against his leg more.

"I like when you're the one hurting me."

His jaw ticks, his grip on me tightens, and he leans up putting space between us.

"Take my cock out," he demands.

I scramble to do it, my hands fiddling with the zipper and button before I finally succeed in pushing his jeans down just enough that he is released. His cock is stiff, throbbing and leaking pre-cum. I swipe my thumb across the tip, rubbing circles.

I look down, seeing how pretty it is. I know they shouldn't be called pretty, but his is. It's thick, long, with veins decorating the shaft in all the right places. It's perfect and I want it inside of me.

I work my hand up and down him. Then he takes a free hand, wraps it around mine and starts helping me work him over. It's lucrative, passionate. Soon he'd starts to push his hips through the vise we created.

He removes my hand, grabbing the base of his cock, and presses the tip against my wet folds, slowly dragging up and down, teasing me as his breaths come out staggered.

Finally he lines himself up perfectly with my entrance and presses his hips forward, letting out a deep, manly groan as he fills me. I'm so full. He is so big. I can feel him in my stomach. I can feel his cock throbbing inside of me, the warmth radiating to my tight walls that clamp down.

I bow into him, looking down again where our hips are connecting, feeling him trying to stretch me out completely. I moan when he slams into me fully, causing my hips to jerk open wider and the strings to gouge into my skin.

"Be a good girl and look me in the eyes while I fuck you," he orders locking eyes with me.

One hand comes toward my face and he swipes my bottom lip with his thumb, before pressing his palm onto my throat and squeezing. His face is so intense, like he's set on making sure no other man will ever make me feel this way. It's gradually becoming harder for me to breathe, the strings constricting around my body like a vise. I was numb from the ecstasy.

My body rocks as he leans over me. I whimper when the tip hits the most sensitive region of my walls. The small upward curve of his cock perfect for stretching me out while simultaneously tickling my g-spot.

"You're so fucking tight," he coos. His chiseled abs assist in pumping into me with little mercy. I can feel every inch of him driving me closer and closer to an orgasm.

I move my hips toward his, meeting each of his heavy thrusts inside of me. We were making our own music. The sounds of our skin connecting to make a symphony of bawdy, obscene noises.

My fingers sink into his shoulders begging silently for my release.

My toes start to curl and just when he goes as deep as he can go, my wall tightens, and my body erupts. I open my mouth to scream but his mouth covers mine, silencing me, devouring my euphoric moans.

He continues to fuck me, but he's slowed down. Taking his time to pull out and go back in, like he's savoring me. With nimble fingers he's started to remove the lights from my body, kissing every red mark, every possible bruise, until I'm free of the binds and he's come.

It was a soft moment, the softest I'd ever seen him. He was worshipping my body. Making me overwhelmed with emotion. My fingers played with his air as he swirled his tongue along my hip bones.

I couldn't imagine a life where I didn't have this. I didn't want to think of a moment where I wouldn't be with him.

He'd sat on his heels tucking himself back into his jeans and examined me for spots left unattended. He wanted to make sure I was okay, that I wasn't hurt. I couldn't help but snicker and think I bet he never did that with other women.

"Malakai, I love you."

I smile nervously, brushing my hair behind my ear. My heart was pounding from the intensity of my orgasm. But it stalls when I see the look in his eyes.

Dread settles in my stomach, an anchor of fear. I lick my dry bottom lip, reaching over for him to pull him back to me, but he stands abruptly.

"Hey, what are you doing?" I ask with my heart in my throat and my forehead wrinkled in confusion.

"Did you hear what I said? I said I love you." I laugh out like the thought of him darting away from me after I just confessed how I felt was impossible.

He wouldn't just be fucking me. That wasn't Kai. I meant more to him.

We meant more to him than that.

"I love—"

"Stop saying that, Charlotte," he snaps, looking over his shoulder at me with a tone that is deafening. Always calm, always together Malakai. The sound means, I'm done talking. But I'm not.

My blood is pumping quickly through my body, leaving me lightheaded as frustration has me throwing my shirt over my naked body. I'd been on cloud nine just a few moments ago and now I was leading with my anger.

"What do you mean stop saying it? It's how I feel. Are you really surprised?"

His back is still to me as he searches for his shirt in such a composed manner that it only pushes me closer to the box of TNT. How can he just look for his clothes right now? Like I don't mean anything, like what I am saying doesn't mean anything.

"Malakai, I'm fucking talking to you, I said that I love——"

"You don't love me. Stop saying it, okay? You don't love me, Charlotte." He turns to face me, looking at me for the first time since I said it. I can see a fury growing in him. He is struggling to sedate the rage inside of him.

He tensed up so tightly I thought he might pass out. There was something malevolent in his eyes. I was going to see a part of him that I'd never seen before. A part of him that refused to be loved, whatever it was that made him believe I couldn't love him.

The part of him he hid from me so well.

The man behind the mask.

Kai

THE ACT of taking someone strong, someone stable, and breaking them was a pastime for me. An activity I derive pleasure from. I want them to feel broken like I did, like Yvonne made me feel. Broken, empty, desolate.

The thing is, I got off on it. I really enjoyed it. Not the sounds of their moans or their faces when they come. I got off on the moment they looked at me with tired eyes and said their safe word. When they couldn't take anymore. Their body physically could have handled hours more, but mentally I'd broken them.

I'd cut their ropes and let them down adamantly, but when they left, I'd jerk off to the image of their face when they couldn't handle it anymore.

I didn't regret it either. Like when a serial killer has no remorse for his victims? I was that way.

But I never wanted this.

I never wanted to break, Charlotte. Not like this. Not at all.

Watching the delicate features of her face fall after the words she spoke with such pure intention had been thrown back in her face by my placid rage.

The words I love you, which would calm any normal person, scare me. They are a one-way path to provoking everything I keep hidden inside of me. A trigger, my trigger.

"I do love you. Stop telling me how I feel! I know how I feel!" she shouts at me, her emotions overflowing only fueling me to meet her intensity.

She steams right up to my face, or tries to, but our height difference makes it difficult. Nonetheless, she wants a fight and I'm not giving her one.

That will only lead to damage. I will hurt her more than she can image because when I snap, I can't control what I say, or worse, what I do. The switch that flips inside of me turns off the Malakai she thinks she loves.

I was already a bastard in every aspect of the word, but I'd taken it a step too far and allowed her, this innocent soul, to fall in love with me. Someone demented.

I bite my tongue, grinding my teeth. I don't want to fight her. I don't want to hurt her anymore. But when she takes another step toward me, reaching her gentle hands out to touch me. When her skin makes contact with my wrists everything shifts.

My vision becomes blurry as the ground beneath my feet shifts. The blood pumping through my body pounds against my eardrums and my skin burns as the walls seem to close in on me.

I can't catch my breath. The rage rips the flesh of my chest apart leaving me exposed.

"Stop, fucking stop!" I shout, jerking my hands away from her grip with a little more force than I needed. She stumbles back from me a bit, staring up at me with wide eyes and wet cheeks.

That's right, cry. Cry because this is who I am, Charlotte.

"You don't—you don't love me! You don't love me! You don't know me!" I step closer to her with every heated word, the weight of her words felt like a chain. A heavy chain and I wanted to rip her to pieces.

She backs up, the closer I get.

"I do know you, Malakai, I do—"

I bend to get in her face, taking another step that presses her into the wall. She leans onto it for support as I slam my fist into the wall behind her. I strike the wall over and over again until I see the bright crimson leak from my knuckles.

"You don't fucking know me, Charlotte. I'm not some knight in shining armor because I happened to keep you from falling into traffic. Do you see these hands?" I shove them in her face just as she flinches.

"Look at me!" I bellow from somewhere deep inside my gut. "You wanted this, now look at me!"

Her body rattles with her cries, or maybe it's from the fear. I'm scaring her. I can see it in her eyes that she is trying to disassociate the man in front of her from the man she'd been fucking earlier.

But she's going to find out they are one and the same.

I'd just gotten better at hiding it.

Hesitantly she looks at my hands, one of which is leaking blood. Her eyes no longer silver but grey. Dull, mournful like clouds over a death.

"These hands hurt people. Do you hear that, Charlotte? I hurt people. You don't know me. You don't know that I was forced to fuck people for money. They used every hole in my body. One, two, three at a time. That these hands you think you're in love with were used to break in new girls. I took people's innocence, stole it from them."

Her forehead wrinkles and her bottom lip quivers as she covers her mouth with both hands.

"Oh God—" she whimpers, not from fear, from pain.

She is hurting for me. She's trying to grasp the fact that I was a prostitute, that I'd had sex with more people by the time I was sixteen than most people have in their entire life. She should be scared right now, repulsed, but instead, she's hurting for me.

My sweet, punk loving girl.

"You don't know about these scars." I grab her wrist with my blood-soaked hand and force her to touch the rubbery, thick scars that brand my back. I try to force my memories into her mind when she grazes them.

I hope she sees me, on my knees, slash after slash. Her moon eyes can't see anything beautiful in this. No. I'm showing her how I see the world and why when I met her I was so fascinated by how she saw things.

"These are whip marks for not completing jobs, for being raped as a child, not making enough money, refusing to let people fuck me! You don't know me!" My chest shook, as I gripped her wrist tighter until she hissed in pain, pulling away from me.

And she looks at me with a face I'll never forget. It'll be charred into me forever, a reminder for why I don't get close to people. It's a look of agony.

Tears, almost as blue as her hair stream down her face, as she shakes her head back and forth not wanting to listen to me, not wanting to believe me.

"No, no, these hands wouldn't hurt me. I know that. I know you wouldn't hurt me because it's me, you wouldn't hurt me," she sobs.

I was gutting myself, ripping out my insides, and laying them out in front of her hoping it would make her see how rotten I am.

She stupidly reaches for my face, and I push her hands away, avoiding her touch. I back away from her, but she chases me, trying to grab ahold of me. My arms, my wrists, my face, and I continue to deny her.

"Please let me touch you. Please, look at me. It's me, Malakai," she pleads, begging me.

I make the mistake of listening to her, looking down at her. She isn't breaking quietly. It's like every atom of her body was hurting at the same time.

She cried like her spirit needed to break loose from her skin, desperate to release an elemental misery on the world.

And her eyes. Fuck, her eyes. It was what the moon looks like when the eclipse is coming to an end. When the sun is leaving her and she can't do anything to stop it.

We had an eclipse, a brief meeting between two people who were not meant to be together forever, no matter how badly they wanted to be.

"Look at me and come back. Come back to me," she whispers with a wet, croaky voice consumed with sadness.

She doesn't want to give up on me. She thinks she can fix me, that I want her to do that.

I can't just break her.

I have to shatter her.

"There is nothing to come back to."

"Don't say that, you don't mean that," she urges, trying to plead with me.

"You were convenient, Charlotte. Do you really think that I'd be with someone like you? Look at you. Didn't you see the women I'm normally with?" I laugh cruelly. "I was fucking you because you were practically begging me for it. I pitied you. That's what you were to me, a pity fuck. I am incapable of loving you."

And that's when I think I became a real monster. When I became Yvonne, because I think I killed her.

Her soul, I killed her soul.

I took the one person on this earth who loved me honestly, purely, without conditions and with no obligations, and I slaughtered her.

She would never forgive me.

Good.

"You did what to my sister?"

I turn to see the other half of the Greene DNA. His fist is balled and he is on a one way path straight for me. I don't bother stopping him. I let him get in my face.

"You son of a fucking bitch, you touched her?" he yells. I see the fist he is swinging coming. I let it make contact with my jaw, hoping it hurt him less than it hurt me. It was solid, but I'd handled worse. Plus, I deserved that.

I hold the place his fist made contact, massaging the soreness that is already starting to develop.

"She was all I had left! The last good thing and look at what you did to her! Her heart was pure and now it's ruined." He shoves my chest, over and over again. The palms of his hands feel like daggers.

He charges at me, ready to swing again, but I bend over and barrel into his stomach. It sends us to the hardwood floor with a bang. I slam my fists into his chest, not wanting to hurt him, but needing to prove my point.

"You ruined her when you started choosing drugs over her. I'm not the only one to blame here. Take some responsibility for yourself, you fucking junkie."

He snarls at me, trying to get out from underneath me like a rabid dog. I only start to get up when I see his nose start bleeding, even though we all know that's not from this altercation.

I let him up, pushing him back.

"Can't even keep that shit out of your nose, can you?" I mock.

He growls, coming toward me again, but Charlotte stops him.

"Em, Em, stop." Stepping between us, clutching his shirt like she might fall over. Like without him standing there she'd fall apart. She'd thrown on her jeans in our fight. She wanted to leave. She needed to.

He stares down at her, seeing the same pain on her face that I saw earlier. He sees that it was more than fucking to her on her face. How could he not? He's her other half.

"Come on, let's go. My apartment has been ready for a little while now. I just thought being around a friend would help. Guess I was wrong."

There is so much animosity in his face that I feel it slice inside me. That cuts. Deeper than I thought it would, losing a friend, because as much shit as we give him, he's my friend. He was.

"Guess so," I reply numbly. I wanted them out of this house, and needed them out before I lost my mind.

Emerson grabs her hand fleeing to the door. He swings it open and I expect them to disappear into a cloud of dust, but Charlotte turns, looking back at me. She stops at the threshold, standing there, staring at me.

"You've fallen far enough already, Malakai. The past doesn't change, people do. I think it's time you forgive yourself."

Then like the last scant minutes before dawn the moon waves goodbye and the sun appears, reminding the world that you can still shine in times of darkness.

SEVENTEEN

When Death Came For Me

CHARLOTTE

*T*he definition of *shock* as described by the Mayo Clinic is a critical condition brought on by the sudden drop in blood flow through the body. Shock may result from trauma, heatstroke, blood loss, an allergic reaction, severe infection, poisoning, severe burns, or other causes.

The other cause is heartbreak.

No one talks about that one because how could something minuscule cause someone to lose oxygen to their organs. How could heartbreak lead to someone's permanent organ damage or death?

Because just as you lose an arm in an accident, you feel the sudden loss of it. Just as you feel the loss of the one you love.

I felt clammy, pale. My stomach was rolling, and I could taste vomit in the back of my throat. More than anything I felt numb to everything that was happening around me.

The sorrow stung so sharply that I'd become used to it as we drove away from a house that once creeped me out but had slowly become home.

I don't believe that the word "pain" does this feeling justice; I don't know that any single word could possibly encompass all of these emotions and the raw intensity of them.

Ripped, torn, shattered, shredded.

Malakai had taken pieces of me, small pieces, until he eventually had all them in his hands. Then like it was nothing but paper, he crumpled it up and threw it over his shoulder with zero regard.

Now what? I'm supposed to keep going?

I'm supposed to forget him?

"Are you going to ignore everything I am saying and continue staring out the window like you're in a nineties music video or are you going to answer my fucking questions, Charlotte?"

Emerson had been yelling at me since we left, beating the dash with his fist, but I'd just sat there not ignoring him, just absorbed in the past. Trying to figure out where I went wrong, where I messed up, how I didn't see that he was using me.

"What would you like me to tell you, Emerson?" I look over at him calmly, so tired of yelling, tired of screaming. My throat was raw. My face was dried up because of all the salt from my tears.

"I want to know when the hell you started sleeping with him and why didn't you tell me?" he says throwing his hands in the air, probably because this is the fourth time he has asked that question since we got in the car.

Sleeping with him was a new development.

I think I've loved him since I was sixteen. Since I gave him my *I Love Chemistry* button.

"Because I knew you'd react like this. Because you're strung out and everything I tell you is going to get blown out of proportion."

"I'm not on drugs, I'm sober—"

"Swear on Mom, swear on Mom and I'll believe you." I snap my eyes to his, daring him to lie on our mother.

"I—" he stutters, he looks back at the road taking a deep breath and letting it out.

"It's just coke."

It's just coke.

It's just a heartbreak.

It's just Alzheimer's.

It's just life.

Just because it's just this or that doesn't make it hurt any less.

"Oh, that's reassuring," I say as I rest my chin in my palm against the window watching the rain drops stick to the glass. I just wanted to take a bath, a scalding hot bath, and go to sleep.

Pretend for a few hours that I didn't just get rejected after telling someone I love them.

Chills race down my arms when I remember what he looked like earlier. His eyes were yellow, like a savage wolf, snarling its teeth at me. I didn't know him. He was right.

I didn't know any of the things he screamed at me, but I knew he wouldn't hurt me. No matter what, he wouldn't hurt me. Not physically anyway.

He'd had the opportunity more than once. Moments before our fight, I was tied with Christmas lights. He had his chance to do his damage, but he didn't. His fingers were gentle, his lips were slow.

I'd—I'd thought he was binding us together.

But apparently I was wrong.

The dull ache returns in my chest as my eyes sting with more tears.

I look over at Emerson, both hands on the wheel, his knuckles bruising from punching Kai. Sloppy curls falling in front of his face, the hollows of his cheeks look a little more sunken, like he hasn't been eating. The runny nose he'd kept wiping with his hoodie sleeve and the purple bags setting underneath his eyes from lack of sleep.

"You can't keep doing this to yourself. You are killing yourself, Em."

He scoffs, "I'm fine."

"You're not fine! Look at you! You are so much better than this. You have so much to offer—"

Like a bomb that had been waiting for the right opportunity, the other man in my life that I love explodes on me.

"I have so much to offer? Like what? Tell me. Because the way I see it, hockey is all I am fucking good at, Charlotte!" he screams, actually screams, booms in an erratic voice. Moving his head back and forth from the road to me in the passenger seat.

"I'm good at fucking things up and hockey. There is no other option for me! How else are we going to afford the facility Mom is living in? Are you going to pay it with your violin? I am busting my ass to make sure none of this falls apart!! I'm not smart like you. I have no degree. It's just hockey! What do you fucking expect from me? What do you want! You want me to pay for all this, right? Then I need cocaine! I can't handle this without it! Do you not see that?"

His face turned crimson, his eyes popped, his neck strained. His words were spat out with the ferocity and single drops of spit hit my face. I remained unblinking against his onslaught.

Unlike Malakai, I'm not sure if Emerson will hurt me or not. The sober Em would die before hurting me, but now? I wasn't sure.

When you have a twin, when you share 50% of their DNA, there is a connection. A bond that is unbreakable, but it's also a bond that means you not only feel your own emotions, you feel theirs too. You are never closer to anybody than when you are in the womb.

Emerson did things to extremes, at different ends of the spectrum than me. But together, we felt whole, like one completed person. All through school I was never an individual. I was always one of the twins. Even though we weren't identical in personality or in looks, we were identical inside. Em was outgoing, collected, cool. I was small, bad-tempered, and bit my nails. But we balanced each other out.

I'd never thought, I never stopped to think about who was there for him when he needed someone. Em was always there for me, always protecting me, being the man of the house since our dad died when we were so young. But he never confided in me, not like I did him.

Even when we were babies he was taking care of me. My mom told me about how I was in the NICU for a week. When I'd become agitated, they'd grab Emerson and lay him down next to me, and my heart rate would calm down immediately.

The only time I've ever seen him like he is now is when he lost his best friend. When Ian died, he cried in my arms all night, but when I woke up he was back to the regular Emerson. Like it never happened. I tried to get him in therapy, to talk to me, but he wasn't listening to me. It was like something inside of him broke, something died in him when Ian did.

Now, he'd been so busy feeling this need to take care of me, of Mom, and no one was checking on him.

I open my mouth wanting to console him when the car jerks to the left. I instantly grab ahold of the dash. My stomach dipping in fear.

"Emerson, slow down," I say.

"It's just a slippery road. I know how to drive or are you going to tell me how to do that now?" he shouts.

And then, my life became a brief collection of in and out.

Maybe the car hit a wet spot or a patch of ice because we'd started spinning like a merry-go-round. Emerson grabbed at the wheel, trying to tug it straight. The anger had left and in its place was fear.

I saw the tree. Tall, wide, looming in the headlights right before we made contact.

I assumed I was dead.

I could taste the coppery liquid pooling in my mouth, thick, goopy. It was stuck to my teeth, wetting my lips. I couldn't breathe, like an elephant was squishing me. The aches and cracks every time I inhaled. The sound of mangled metal and squealing tires. Burnt rubber and smoke became my air.

When the spots in my vision appeared, that's when the kaleidoscope of my life began.

Except I wasn't relieving them. I was watching them from above.

Emerson and I played hide and seek with our Mom in the park. The same time Emerson fell from the jungle gym and broke his arm. We'd gotten ice cream after they put a cast on it, and I had signed it, "Next time you won't jump. Love, the smart half."

My mom is reading to us in our bunk beds. Emerson got the top, I was on the bottom. My sheets were dinosaurs. Em's friends had said it was weird for a girl to like boy stuff. Emerson said it was cool.

The first time I touched a violin. The first time I played.

Winning the science fair, helping Mom lug pounds of ice

upstairs to the bathroom for Em after games, losing my virginity, Ian's funeral, Mom's diagnosis. My life had become nothing but a film reel.

I was fading away from them. My memories were dwindling until he showed up.

The way he flips the pages like he's reading the newspaper, his hazel eyes, seeing him play in the yard with Cerberus from my bedroom window, my performances for him, getting to see him paint.

I felt washed with gratitude. Of being able to experience the life I did. Of having a mother that loved me, a twin that would do anything for me, and Malakai, a man who may not have loved me, but showed me what love could be.

I was lucky. I was dying with memories.

I hoped, more than anything, that this is what my mom saw when her time came.

I could hear the sound of static. My ears were buzzing as a small ball of light starts to lead me away.

And I could hear my mom. I could hear her reading Emily Dickinson.

"We passed the School, where Children strove. At Recess, in the Ring. We passed the Fields of Gazing Grain. We passed the Setting Sun."

My grazing grain was my family, and my setting sun was Kai.

Emily was right, that life, when it's gone, it's gone for good.

EIGHTEEN

Without Color

KAI

I stood leaning on the doorway of my most cherished room. My sanctuary. The safe haven in my home holding a cup of steaming coffee.

The sun was shining through the windows gifting me with natural light to admire the havoc I wrecked on my studio last night.

Ripped canvases, shredded pieces of sketchbook paper, thrown brushes, paint splattered everywhere, tables flipped, chairs broken. I had destroyed it all. All the paintings of naked women, my ideas for future murals. There wasn't a single piece of art left.

I spent years creating the art inside of that room.

It took twenty minutes to destroy it all.

Cerberus was sniffing around, ears bents and sad eyes. Even he knew I was hurting, that this had hurt me.

I stepped inside, looking around. I flipped over canvases, picked up salvageable paints, and tried to clean up some of it. But even if I could, I didn't want to. There was nothing in here that I wanted to recreate or save.

I set my coffee down, placing my hands onto the cracked wooden table, dropping my head and taking a moment to collect myself.

There hadn't been one second of sleep last night, just me, fuming around the house. The art room was wrecked. I'd busted the mirror in my bedroom, threw shit around my kitchen. I was on a warpath to cause as much destruction to myself as possible.

But nothing was making me feel better, nothing was calming me down. So I wanted to dismantle the root of the problem.

I'd torn up the steps, slamming the door to her room open. This was her fault. She's the one who moved into my house. The one who made me touch her. She's the one who came into my life and made me think I could have normal things.

Why was I wrecking my shit when I should've been destroying hers.

Except I couldn't.

When the door opened and I saw her space, I wasn't angry anymore. Inside her room were pieces of her. As if what happened last night didn't actually happen. Her violin was on her bed, bow laid haphazardly beside it. Textbooks and sheet music scattered across the floor.

And the old MP3 player that lays next to her headphones.

She would lie on the ground, close her eyes, and listen to music. She did it often. I wasn't sure why she preferred the floor, but I'd learned early on not to question how she did things. It would only confuse you more.

I had walked into the room, sat down, placed the headphones over my ears, and looked down at the MP3 player at the most recent song. It was labeled underneath *Audition Options* and a sad smile came across my face.

There was no doubt in my mind that she would've killed that audition. They would be stupid not to give her a spot, because Charlotte was that talented. I laid on the ground, pressed play, and closed my eyes.

The female vocalist starts out slow, sounding so much like Charlotte. The same ache, the weathered nature of it was so similar, they made you feel it. Every single word, you felt it in your soul. It resonated in you, stuck with you.

I wanted to text her, to tell her that this was the song she needed to perform. Anything else just wouldn't work. Except I'm stuck lying on her floor, listening to this woman, and there are tears leaking from my shut eyes.

When I open my eyes, I'm back in the art room, staring at the ground.

Staring at a small, circular object.

A button that reads *I Love Chemistry*.

I reach down, pick it up, and rub my thumb across the top of it. I knew I had kept it. I just thought I'd lost it years ago.

Even when she leaves, she's still right here.

My doorbell rings, reminding me that I have to return to real life today. I slide the metaphorical mask over my face and jog to the front door. I scoop my giant duffle bag up off the ground as I open the door to Nico.

"Ready to get your ass kicked?" He smiles like a golden retriever. I'm not sure I can make it through today.

"Ready," I say, closing the door, and walking toward Nico's car that is carrying Bishop and Valor in the backseat.

Valor's window is down and she is smiling at me.

"Where's Dalia?" I ask not noticing a car seat anywhere.

"She's in the car with my dad. He's spent more time with our daughter than we have," she jokes.

I nod, forcing a smile.

I think this is how people who get drunk feel the next day when they have to go to church. Trying to fake emotions when really all they want to do is throw up.

I toss my stuff into the trunk, feeling my phone vibrate in my back pocket. Considering everyone I talk to is in front of me, I'm not sure who could be calling at seven in the morning.

"Hello?"

"Is this Malakai Petrov?"

I hold the phone between my shoulder and ear as I slam the trunk closed.

"Yes, this is him, can I help you?" I ask.

"Mr. Petrov, you are the emergency contact listed for Emerson Greene. I've called to inform you that he has been involved in a car accident. He's doing fine. He's gotten stitches in his forehead and—"

"Charlotte Greene? Was she in the car with him? His sister, how is she? Is she okay?" I interrupt her after she tells me that Em is fine.

Charlotte was in the car with him when he left. She looked at me one last time. I let her leave and get in the car with him.

"Sir, I'm sorry I can't give out information about patients that haven't listed you as an immediate family member."

My heart stops. It stops beating completely and my body begins to hurt. She's a patient. It hurts in places I didn't even know I had. I fall into the car, placing my hand on the roof for support.

Adrenaline floods my system. It pumps and beats like it's trying to escape. It's moving so fast I almost vomit. I can't let the last thing I told her be a lie. I can't let her die thinking she didn't mean anything to me.

She deserves better than that.

You think you have time, that you have forever, and the last time isn't really the last time.

"What did he put me down as?" I ask with the bitter taste of coffee in my throat.

"His brother."

IF NICO TOLD me to calm down one more time, I was going to throw him through a wall. My knees were bouncing rapidly as I rested my elbows on them. My hands covering my mouth, ignoring everyone's stares.

I was told to wait for the doctors after security nearly threw me out for trying to go through doors I wasn't allowed to enter. My mind had become a drawing board of possibilities. Remaining optimistic wasn't my thing, I prepared for the worst at all times.

Except how do you prepare for someone to walk out and tell you that the person you cared most for was dead?

I would no longer hear her play, I'd never see her blue hair laid beneath me again, never hear her laugh, lose to her in Jeopardy. We'd run out of time. She was out of time.

I feel a hand on my leg, looking down to see Riggs is holding onto my knee. She squeezes it tightly.

"Whatever happens, this family has you. Your family always has you, just like you had us."

I look up at her, remembering a time when I was the one holding her from breaking down. All of these people, I'd seen them at their worst.

I'd slept on Nico's couch for a week after Riggs left him.

I'd watched Valor get her heart broken for the first time. Then I'd consoled Bishop when he would come home drunk because he missed her.

I had been there for their darkest moments, and now, they sat here, witnessing mine.

When the door opened to the waiting room and a short man wearing scrubs walked in, I stood abruptly. I'm sure me charging at him would have spooked him, so I approached him calmly when he said.

"Greene?"

I swallow my fear.

"Charlotte Greene, how is she?"

"I'm sorry. I am only allowed to give information on Emerson."

I'd been told that multiple times since I got here. I'd been told thrice that Em was fine, only seven stitches on his forehead and bruising. I didn't need any more information on him.

"Emerson is doing—"

"*Хорошо*! I know. You've told me. You know what's not fine? Charlotte Ophelia Greene! Who has no living family besides a mother with Alzheimer's and a twin in a hospital bed. A girl who is alone, a girl who only has me right now. I couldn't give a fuck less about your hospital protocol. How is she?" I'm not yelling, but my voice was thunderous. My stance was rigid. All I wanted was answers.

The doctor sighs, taking his scrub cap off slowly.

"She is still in surgery, it—it..." he stutters, trying to find the right words. "It doesn't look very good."

You can never prepare for this. There is nothing in the world worse than this.

"Metal from the car punctured her femoral artery and one of her broken ribs punctured her lung. One would be tough, but not fatal, but with both." He gives me a look of pity.

"She coded in the ambulance," he continues making this nightmare more real.

She coded, she died.

She died thinking she was convenient. Thinking she wasn't enough. She died not knowing that she'd been the only woman I'd ever willingly had sex with, that she was the only person I'd let touch me the way she did. That she was the only person I let see my art, the only person I—I—

The only person I've ever loved.

"They were able to successfully resuscitate her, but when she came in she'd lost a severe amount of blood that caused her to go into cardiac arrest. They are working to repair the lung and the artery. I will try to keep you updated. You can come back to see Emerson whenever you are ready," he finishes, raising his hand to my shoulder and squeezing it, before giving me a curt nod and exiting.

I force the pain I'm feeling down, covering it with fury. I was going to kill him.

"Malakai, don't—" But I'm already tearing through the hallway, searching for his room. He may be fine right now, but when I was done, he wouldn't be.

When I find the room, I bust inside speaking before I even lay eyes on him. My friends had never seen this, this frantic side of me, the one that was brought out by pain.

"Is this enough? Is this what it takes? Killing your sister? Is that what it's going to take to make you sober? Because if you're gonna continue, I'm putting a bullet between your eyes," I steam as I stampede toward him.

I grip the material of his nightgown, pulling him out of the bed a little and shaking him like a rag doll. I bare my teeth. I was angry, desperate, regretful. I wanted him to fight me back, to fuel my anger, but when I looked at him, he already seemed lifeless.

"Go ahead, kill me, I'm rotting anyway," he says with a deathly calm voice, like all that's left is skin and bones, no soul. He'd given up. This was the last straw, losing her. There would be two roads, either he kills himself or he gets sober.

I want to hate him, to loathe every fiber of his being, but I can't. Because half of him is the woman I love and the other half is my best friend.

"I will never forgive you for this." I shoved him back onto the bed and he grunts. I was breathing hard, the needles in my throat choking me.

"I will never forgive you unless you go to rehab, because that's what she would've wanted. Either you go or I tell the league you're on drugs. That's your choice."

He looks out the hospital window at the slushy snow that's falling, not moving, not saying anything. Just staring.

I wonder if he feels empty. If he feels gutted without her. It pisses me off that he feels worse than I do because she is half of him. She's a part of him forever.

The rest of our friends come inside, timidly waiting to make sure we aren't screaming at each other. Riggs walks over to the side of the bed, wrapping her arms around his neck, and hugging him tightly.

He turns, seeing all the people here for him.

"Rehab or you're done," I say again.

Another beat of silence passes before he speaks.

"When we were twelve, Charlie fell in love with a blue parakeet at a pet store. She begged Mom to let her have it and it's hard to tell her no." He returns his gaze to the window, his Adam's apple bobbing.

"She fed it, cleaned the cage twice a day, talked to it. She tried to get it to sleep with her one night." He laughs a little as his face becomes wet with tears.

"I held her while she cried when she found the bird dead after school. Then she orchestrated a funeral in our backyard and started dying her hair blue. She can't even look at birds now, because with Charlie..." he trails off, choking on his emotions, crying hard.

"She loves hard, with everything in her. She gives everything to the people she loves, and I think she would've loved you all. I know she would have."

He doesn't bother wiping the tears from his face, just looks directly at me and says,

"Rehab, for her."

The rest of them walk to him hugging him, rejoicing in the fact he's okay. However, I can't stay in this room.

So I step out, opening the door and standing next to it allowing my back to press into the wall. I slide down, hitting the hospital floor with a thud. I hold my hands in front of my face. I press my fingers into my eyes. They feel heavy from the lack of sleep, or maybe from the grief.

I sit here, letting the sounds of nurses and machines fizzle out. I drag my hands down my face to my mouth before folding them and joining them together in front of my lips.

The last time I was doing this, I had fresh bandages on my back to keep the bleeding from leaking onto my clothes. The church had been empty. It was only me, a child on my knees begging for help.

I'm an adult now. A grown man, who hasn't been inside of a church in years. And here I am, trying to believe in something, anything that'll spare her.

"I've done nothing to deserve this favor I'm going to ask," I whisper into my hands, shutting my eyes.

"But this favor isn't for me. It's for her. She's a good person. She deserves a longer life. She needs to fall in love with someone who is worthy of her. She needs to play in an orchestra. She needs to be a mom because the world needs all the good mothers we could use. So please, please I will," my voice breaks, "I will do whatever you want, just don't take her yet."

Charlotte had taught me that I was capable of love, that all I needed was the right person. She'd taken a chance on me, and I spit in her face. So now, I was willing to take a chance and pray for her.

Maybe I've wanted to love all along, but I wasn't able to because my soul was in a different room and they didn't have the key. She had it though. As if something had put it in her pocket the day we bumped into each other when she was sixteen.

Someone slides down the wall next me and soon there is an arm around my shoulder, heavy and firm. I turn to Nico, who's looking at me with understanding, no pity, just empathy. There is a pause in time, when I forget that I'm the mysterious guy. That I'm the one who doesn't say much about himself. The one who protects his feelings from people so that this doesn't happen.

I forget I'm that guy, and my head falls onto Nico's shoulder. I fall like the last domino. Pride isn't something I can afford at the moment, so I let the tears I wanted to cry when she told me she loved me, free.

I was afraid Charlotte was chains, but she was really just trying to free me of them.

"She doesn't know I love her. She died and she doesn't know."

Isn't it a tragedy that we can love something that death can touch?

NINETEEN

God's Messenger

CHARLOTTE

*D*ying is painless. It's living that hurts.

My body throbbed. My head felt like I was underwater. The Sahara Desert found a home in my throat and I needed water. So badly that before I even opened my eyes I was croaking,

"Wa-wat-water," I whisper hoarsely.

I wasn't even sure if there was anyone in here or if I'm even alive. I will say that if I'm dead, it's bullshit that I'm still hurting this badly.

With more strength than I thought I had, I willed my eyes to open. They cracked like bottles of wine, attacked admittedly by the light. I raise my arm to my forehead, shielding my eyes from the intrusive brightness.

"Here."

Then I feel something against my dry lips. I stick my tongue out feeling the straw, and hoping whatever is at the bottom of this cup doesn't kill me. I take small drinks at first making sure I can handle that much liquid at one time.

I down the water until I hear the straw spurting signaling that there is no more.

I try opening my eyes again, letting them flutter open, taking my time to adjust to the light. When they can stay open without burning, I shift my gaze to the voice that offered me the water.

Stunned when I see him.

I think the car accident was less painful than seeing him again.

Can you both rejoice that you are seeing the last person you saw before you died and in pain because it's the man who broke your heart moments prior?

Wait, car accident.

"Em, where is he? Is he okay?" I ask desperately, looking around the room to see if anyone else is in here. If my twin is here.

"Charlotte, he's fine. Just a few stitches. He's more worried about you. We all are," Malakai says, petting my hair with his hand.

I take a breath of relief, thankful for airbags or whatever it is that saved his life. I eye Kai up and down. Hating how beautiful he is. Hating that he looks like he did the first day I met him.

Jeans and a hoodie that I want to snuggle into, because when he hugs me it's like falling into a cloud. He absorbs me, allows me to fall into him.

The purple bags he is sporting bring out the green in his eyes and his hair needs brushed.

"You look like shit," I blurt out feeling the need to fill the silence. The more I have time to think, the more nauseous I get. I feel haunted by his words.

They are repeated punches in the gut.

He scoffs out a chuckle and I join him in a short laugh. Laughs that turn quiet. Neither of us saying anything. Maybe he's just here for Emerson's sake, maybe he's thinking of something to say, maybe this, maybe that.

"You're the only person I know who would make a joke after dying," he says shaking his head at me.

"I died?" I ask, swallowing the cotton in my throat. Not many people know what that's like. To be told you died.

I don't remember dying. I remember the moments before but not death. I think that's because the Grim Reaper is actually a sweet man who got dealt the wrong hand.

He clears his throat, looking at me with a broken look in his eyes, like he is in pain.

"You died. Twice," he starts, his hazel eyes growing watery with tears, actual tears. "Once in the ambulance, once on the table. Then you came back, you came back." He clenches his jaw, as two tear drops fall.

"Like I should have come back to you."

Only love could hurt this bad. There is nothing on this earth that hurts worse than this. This wound that hasn't even healed that he marked into me. I want to be upset, angry with him. I want to deny my heart the luxury of loving him.

But I can't because Malakai Pertrov isn't someone you spend lifetimes trying to forget, but never can because he isn't just a memory.

He is a song. He is a painting. A sunrise. He is pain. He is love.

He is love and you don't just forget an emotion like that.

"I meant when I said, I'm incapable of loving you."

I don't bother trying to fake my emotions. I don't bother to be strong. I cry because it hurts and it hurts because it was real. I know what we had was real.

"Why—Why are you telling me this?" I mumble.

He tilts his head, looking at me like you would a small puppy or child. He wipes the tears beneath my eyes away.

"Because I'm not capable of loving you the way you deserve, but I have the nerve to love you anyway."

I raise my quivering hands to my mouth, overpowered by the strength of this moment.

He ducks his head, pausing for a second before looking back up.

"They say every seven years your body destroys all its cells and creates new ones. Every seven years I vowed to celebrate that trans-formation, to have skin they never disturbed. Then they told me you were dying, and—" His words get stuck in his throat, but he still continues, intent on saying his piece.

"And the first thing I thought of was how miserable I was going to be in seven years because I will then have a body you haven't touched."

He grabs my hand, covering it with both of his. The warmth of his skin encasing mine.

"I don't want to have a life without you in it. I don't want to hear music that you're not playing. I don't want a body that hasn't felt your love, Moon Eyes."

Moon Eyes.

His Moon Eyes.

My Fallen Angel.

We both deserve happy endings. After everything we'd been through, we deserved happy endings. I just couldn't give him one.

I love him. Denying that to myself would be naive. But allowing him to make it up to me in this capacity is also just as naive.

I pull my hand from his, chewing the inside of my cheek as I will myself to speak. Not sure if it's my chest refusing to let me or my heart.

"Since my mom was diagnosed all I've wanted is to remember, to hold onto this life." I wave my hands in a circle, giving a wistful smile.

"These memories I create, I have been clinging to. And the other night, when I thought I'd be making one of the most important memories, you made me want to forget for the first time."

"I know—" he starts, but I shake my head, tears choking me,

"I don't wanna live like that, Kai. I don't want to live a life I will want to forget one day. I don't want someone who loves me because I almost died. I want someone to love me because I make them want to live."

He wants to argue, but my exhausted face tells him I'm not up for the fight.

"I'm scared that you feel this way now and a month from now you won't feel the same. You'll blow up on me like you did before. I can't love someone who is afraid of letting me love them."

Fear is death's cruel twin brother and apparently, I was having a family reunion because their cousin heartbreak was sitting on the bed next to me.

Silence passes between us. Painful silence that allows my words to sink in. He looks so tired, like he hasn't slept, because he probably hasn't.

I want to take it back. I want to tell him to hell with being scared, I love you. But I can't. I don't want him to be like he was the other night. He hates himself more when he's like that. I don't want to be the reason he hates himself.

Another beat before he stands up, leaning down and laying his lips on my forehead. He stays there for longer than necessary, but I let him because I need it too.

"You were just a boy. You are not a monster," I whisper.

"Try not to trip over anyone else's paintings. There's a lot of graffiti in Chicago, Moon Eyes."

Then he's gone. Leaving the hospital room with his hands tucked into his pockets and hood up. Like he was never there.

I'm sobbing, hysterically, crying so hard and my lungs feel like they are on fire. I grab the pillow behind me, burying my face in it, trying to muffle my cries.

I have no reason to feel the way I do right now. I have no right to be hurting, to be crying when he told me what I wanted to hear. He told me what I needed, but I don't want him to love me because he feels guilty.

I want him to love me because he can't live without me. Because he can't breathe without me.

If it's anything less than that, then he deserves better and so do I.

TWENTY

So Much for My Happy Ending

CHARLOTTE

"You sure you're okay to drive?" Emerson asks me from the passenger seat.

I look over at him, the bruising on his face has started to disappear from his skin. The only thing remaining was the scar above his eyebrow from the stitches. There was something peaceful in how he looked right now.

He seemed tired, but he was done fighting his addiction. He was ready to get the help he needed.

"I'm fine to drive, Em. I'm feeling good as new, just a little sore," I reassure him.

It had been two weeks since the accident. Emerson had been released a few days after and had told me he'd decided to go to rehab. A ninety-day program, but he wanted to wait until I was out of the hospital and on my feet before leaving.

I wasn't sure how it would work with the Fury, but three days ago an article was published telling Fury fans that Emerson Greene would be recovering from an undisclosed injury that had required surgery.

It'd also been two weeks since I'd heard from Malakai, well personally. He'd passed messages to Emerson to tell me. Like the fact he'd moved all of my things into Emerson apartment, and apparently friends of his had stocked the fridge for me.

I almost wished he was a dick after. I wanted a reason to hate him. A reason not to run to him. I'd been honest with Kai. I was honest with myself. I needed to heal. I needed to make sure Emerson healed.

Maybe we were forever, our forever just wasn't right now.

"You going to be okay?" I ask as we pull into the rehab center, looking at the expensive building that looked more like a hotel than a rehab facility.

"Are *you* going to be okay?" he returns the question.

I sigh with an eye roll. I reach over, throwing my arms over his shoulders and hugging him to my body. I hold him there for a minute, because he's my brother. Because he's all I have, and I want him to be better. I need him to be better.

"I think it's time you start thinking of yourself. You've been thinking about Mom and me for too long. Take this time for you. I'm going to be okay. I'll be right here waiting."

He holds the back of my head, squeezing me. "Thank you for not giving up on me, Charlie."

Giving up on him is like giving up on me.

We stay there for a moment, just hugging each other like we did when we were children. When I'd have nightmares and he would get on the bottom bunk with me. Always protecting me.

My brother was a drug addict, but he was also an amazing brother. A great hockey player, a guy with a contagious laugh, someone who is loyal to a fault, and I'm lucky to have him in my life.

When I pull from the hug, he is holding a CD between us, wiggling it.

I raise my eyebrow, trying to snatch it out of his hands, but he pulls it from me.

"I don't ask a lot from you, Char. But I need you to do something for me while I'm gone." He places the CD into my hands.

"I need you to be happy. That's all I've ever wanted for you,

Charlie. So, whatever you choose to do, don't be afraid to be happy."

I'm confused and insanely curious about what is on this thing now. He grabs his bags, gets out of the car, and walks to the doors of the center.

"Behave yourself, Em!" I yell at him.

He turns, walking backwards, and shoots me a playful wink. "Never."

Then, he's gone. I'm both excited and full of sorrow. I'm happy that I don't need to worry about where he is every second of the day for the next ninety days, but I'm also sad that I don't have to do that.

I look at the CD, the words *play me* are written with a sharpie, so I do as instructed and pop it into the stereo system pulling out of the center to drive back home. I wait patiently for track one to play but when I'm met with nothing but silence I go to press the skip button.

"Moon Eyes."

It stops me. His voice feels like aloe on a burn. It's smooth and heals all my aches. No matter what happens in the future I don't ever want to forget the way he says my name. I clutch the steering wheel with both hands, trying to pay attention to traffic, but hanging on the edge of my seat for his next sentence.

"I'd like to show you something. So, if you'd like to see it, all you have to do is follow the clues on the CD. Do you remember the first day we met? I do. You had striped socks and the sole of your shoe was busted open. Even then you were a mess, but I like you that way. It was the first time someone had seen me for who I was, a boy who'd been through something painful. Go there. Walk to the wall, there is something there for you, then change to track two."

Life is about choices. Good or bad. Right or wrong. Left or right.

My choice to replay the track in order to hear his voice again. My choice to drive to the spot where I'd seen his first mural. It was still there, a little faded, but still beautiful in its own right.

I'd gotten out of my car like he asked and when I walked to the wall there was a blue sticky note. His neat handwriting printed nicely in black ink. I pick it off, reading the message:

Touch has a memory. -John Keats
Yours is my greatest, M.

My fingers still remember how his rigid scars felt on his back. I'd known something bad had happened to get them, but no one can prepare you for something tragic like that. How someone can steal the innocence of a child.

A child who I know was smart, who loved to read, and never deserved the harsh treatment he was dealt. He didn't deserve that. No one does.

Fear. That's what keeps me from him.

Fear. That one day he will realize I am not enough for someone as amazing as him. That when he learns to forgive and grows, he will see I was just a stepping stone to someone better.

Fear. That we might create a beautiful life together, with children of our own, memories of our love, and I will be passed the Alzheimer's gene and forget him completely.

I get back in my car, laying the sticky note on the seat, and pressing track two before my brain can talk me out of it.

"When I moved to the states with my aunt, I'd realized she had a fascination with Matryoshka dolls. I think it's because they represent fertility in Russian culture, and she was unable to have kids of her own. I would love for you to meet her. She's the only mother I've ever known. Even though her eyes are green and yours are grey, you see the world the same. Go to the place where you first had Pirozhki. The first night I ever wanted to kiss someone more than I wanted to breathe. Go inside, they will handle the rest."

I played for him that night.

There was something about him that made me think he would accept me. He wouldn't critique the song choice or the way my bow went across the strings. He would appreciate the art. It was when he stopped seeing me as a sixteen-year-old and started seeing me as a woman.

There was so much I wanted to know about him. What made him the stoic, aloof man he was. Driving to the restaurant put me back there. I could still see the suit he was wearing, the few pieces of hair that fell in front of his face, and the smiles he tried to hide.

It smelled the same, like onions and fish. It doesn't sound pleasant but I actually liked it. It had a homey feeling. I remember thinking that I bet this is what Kai's home smelled like. Never suspecting that his home was a place of abuse.

As soon as the host saw me, he reached behind the desk and retrieved a set of dolls like the ones Malakai mentioned. I assume Kai told him a girl with blue hair would be coming in, considering how fast the man recognized me.

I accept the gift, walking back to my car before opening it. When I get to the final doll, I open it and inside is something folded. My fingers work to unfold it, seeing that it's a picture. One of me.

I'm spinning in the snow in Malakai's front yard, Cerberus is in the corner of the photo, and there is a smile on my face. At the bottom is Kai's handwriting:

I didn't know happiness until I met you. -M

There were other boys after meeting Kai, they tried to under-stand me, but I'd fallen in love with his soul that day. They couldn't take what was already taken.

I'd let them in superficially. We would go on dates. Have sex. Hang out. But Kai was always in the back of my mind, some days more than others.

We always seemed to be in the same place, but still managed to be in different time zones. The electricity of our connection sparked. We had chemistry from the day I gave him that button, but our fears snuffed it out like a power company turning your lights off.

We had always been love, never ready for it.

I pressed the next button and listened for my directions.

"Last destination, Charlotte. No clues, just an address. I know you said I had to forgive myself, but what you don't know is loving you is doing that. Allowing myself to love you, being able to love you, it's the only forgiveness I need. I'll be waiting, I hope you show."

I heard the directions, plug them into my GPS, and start the drive there. The closer I got the more I started to worry I was headed in the wrong direction. The area was being remodeled.

Buildings that had been torn down and some that were getting face-lifts.

I was going to turn around, but I'm glad I didn't because I would've missed the brick building with my face on the side of it. It was one of the places that had been remodeled, new brick had been laid and now the left side of it was decorated with spray paint.

I stopped my car and get out to walk over to the artwork. My heart was becoming claustrophobic inside of my chest, banging on the walls wanting to see what was going on outside.

It was unbelievable.

There was me from the waist up, painted monochromatic. Different shades of blue created the structure of my face and hair. I'd never considered myself beautiful until right now. Because he painted it.

My violin in near perfect detail was perched on my shoulder, painted in white. Behind me was a tall man, highlighted in spots of grey and white with two scars tearing down his back. The wings he'd lost had been forged into a bow, the same bow I was playing with.

Except it's not just a man, it's Kai.

Kai had given his wings for me to play.

"I still owed you a painting for giving me a name, right?"

I turn around, meeting his gaze. His hair is down, the wind catching it. I think he knows I like it down. He's using it against me right now.

Do you know when you've been gone all day? Running errands, working out, working in general, and you don't get home until late in the evening. When you finally stick your key in the door, twist, maybe jiggle the knob a bit, and then you walk inside.

The smell of your home hits you and this weight falls off your shoulders? It doesn't matter if the house is a mess or spotless, you're just thankful to be home.

That's how I feel right now.

Thankful to be near him.

"Just a few years late."

He walks toward me slowly, deliberately, and I stay rooted in place. He looms over me.

"I guess I finally found my muse," he says in a breath.

My heart skips.

"I thought pain was your muse?" I ask, tilting my head.

He nods, "Pain was the past. Pain is an emotion." He lays a hand on my cheek, holding my gaze.

"You are my muse. You are my celestial wonder, my cosmic violinist, my moon-eyed girl, and I am in love with you. You gave my life color where they had left me grey, and I'd like to give you a life worth remembering. Will you let me do that?"

I raise my hand to his on my face, running my thumb along the bruised skin. I hold him there, not wanting to let go.

"Does that mean I get to leave my clothes on your steps and feed Cerberus peanut butter?"

He laughs, airy and light. Like the clouds that hovered above him are gone and the murky water in his lungs has finally drained.

"As long as I can kiss you right now. You can do whatever you want, Charlotte. It's your world, babe. I'm just lucky to live in it."

And I let him.

I let him kiss me because sometimes you don't need a knight or a prince. Sometimes you just need a man willing to paint you a mural and tell you that you're made of cosmic dust. That your eyes look like the moon, and your love heals him.

Sometimes it's just a man.

Epilogue

THREE MONTHS LATER

Kai

*W*hen do you realize you've made it in life?

Is it when you make a certain amount of money? When you achieve a dream you've been working for? When do get to look in the mirror and say,

'You did it.'

I used to think it was when I could look at myself and not see the kid who was raped. When I could see myself as something more than someone who's been abused. I thought if I could just get there, if I could cover it up and move forward, it would disappear. I would make it.

But that's not it.

That's not making it.

Making it is looking into the living room from the kitchen and watching the love of your life roll around on the floor kicking one of your best friend's ass while everyone else watches and cheers around them. This place is filled with teammates. Family. Our family.

Bishop didn't believe her when she said she was a black belt in Jiu-Jitsu. I had my doubts until she'd come to work out with me. So now, Bishop was in a headlock, tapping out while everyone gave him hell.

I took a sip of my beer, leaning on the island, smiling as Charlotte rolls off the ground raising her hands in the air cheering.

My girl was a badass.

She could very well whip my ass if she wanted, sat through tattoos like it was a massage, and yesterday I'd watched her soak her blistered fingers in salt water then play the next day.

I'd never met someone as gentle yet rebellious.

She was stunning on the outside, but she was also beautiful within, from the love she gives to her ideas and creative mind. I wanted to be a better man because of her.

"You need any help picking this up?"

I look over at Emerson who'd put on some muscle since the last time I'd seen him. His normal skin tone had returned and there wasn't a bloodshot eye in sight. He looked healthy.

I slap his shoulder. "I've got it all handled man, you headed out?" I ask motioning to his jacket in hand.

It makes me a tad nervous letting him leave early, but I have to have faith in him. Faith that he is going to stick with his program and not relapse.

"Yeah I've got to get up early. I have to do community service for damaging the guardrail I went through. There is a kids' club. They want me to help coach. The first day is tomorrow," he tells me, shrugging the jacket over his shoulders.

Emerson got home from rehab yesterday, and we had thrown him a welcome home party. Well, Charlotte did.

She'd been bouncing around trying to keep it a secret. She sucks at secrets. But from the look on Emerson's face when we had said surprise, my girl kept quiet for once.

"Thank you, man. For making good on your promise," Emerson says.

He is referring to the promise I made him in the hospital. That if he gave me the green light, I would make her happy.

I was determined to keep making good on that promise for the rest of my life.

"Thank you for helping yourself." We give each other a hug before he leaves the party.

I thank everyone for coming, hugging them as they head to the door. I laugh at Bishop who is massaging his neck and Valor who is rocking Dalia.

I'd accepted the fact that I wasn't going to get rid of these people. They were my family. All of them.

Riggs had convinced me to attend therapy, which I do regularly now, not because I enjoy talking to some random guy, but because Charlotte thought it helped me, which made her happy.

I didn't want therapy, did I need it? Probably. But touching her, seeing her smile, being around her was the best remedy.

When the last person exited my house, I looked around for my punk rock girl, but she wasn't anywhere to be seen.

"Charlotte?" I call around, but she doesn't answer.

I furrow my eyebrows, taking the steps, worry settling in my stomach until I see a pair of red lace panties on the steps.

I scoop them up with a wolfish grin, hearing her hum from our bedroom. I know what she's doing. It's the same thing she does every single night I'm home.

Even when I'm at away games, she calls me and asks me to do one thing for her.

I jog up the steps, heading into our room that is thankfully clean. I let her keep her spare bedroom as her work space. She can keep all that mess in her room, as long as she sleeps next to me at night, I don't care.

I grab the book from my nightstand and walk into the bathroom. She's covered in bubbles, her black nail polished toes peeking out of the end, and her blue hair is thrown up into a bun.

My chair is still next to the tub, where it stays.

"Soon I'm going to be out of poems, Moon Eyes," I joke as I sit down, looking over at her as she places her hands on the side, resting her chin on the edge.

"Then I guess you'll have to start writing me some originals."

I roll my eyes. She makes me read to her, almost every night.

Always John Keats. Because as she tells me, *"Romantics read Keats, Malakai Adrian, and we are romantics now."*

I wouldn't call myself a romantic. I just love doing certain things that she finds sweet.

I love drawing her, sketching her when she isn't paying attention to me. When she is sleeping or playing. Drawing the Cupid's bow on her lips or the curve in her nose. Even drawing her while she is in the kitchen, which are rare moments, but she's learning.

And if there's one thing I have learned about her these past months, she's a quick learner.

I was more than okay having normal, vanilla sex with Charlie, but she knew I needed something else every once in a while.

She explored my tastes with ferocious curiosity, read books, looked up knots and binds she wanted to try. I loved her even more for that. Because she knew what I needed and wasn't afraid to give it to me.

"Thank you for this. I know you hate parties," she mutters as steam floats up around her.

"Who said that?" I draw back faking offense.

"Babe," she says in a dull tone, giving me 'the look.' "You hate strangers, and loud social settings make you cranky," she says scrunching her nose as if it was common knowledge. Which I guess, to her it is.

She watches me like a hawk most days. Not because she thinks I'm doing something wrong, but because she just enjoys watching me.

"They don't make me cranky. I just prefer to be alone with you," I correct her, leaning over and placing a kiss on her forehead.

I read to her. I feel her eyes watching my mouth pronounce words and read about love. She loves long poems, ones with alliteration because I roll my Rs hard, and apparently she likes that.

I read to her because it's what makes her happy. I want to be the man who reads to her every day for the rest of our lives. The old man that is still hopelessly in love with his woman.

"I forgot my violin today. All the way to practice and realized it I didn't have it," she says interrupting my second poem. I put the book down, kneeling on the ground so I am face to face with her.

Taking her small face in my hands, so she tilts into my touch.

I love that. I love how every time I touch her, she melts into me. Doesn't matter if it's a hug, or if I wrap an arm around her in bed, she automatically curls into me.

"Charlie, it happens, normal people forget." A tear falls down her cheek and I catch it.

Every time she forgets something, her keys, her wallet, she has this moment. Where she freaks out and wonders if it's the Alzheimer's gene kicking in.

"But——"

"But nothing. I don't know what will happen in ten years, Charlotte. No one does. But I know I love you and that you are brave. You are brave, my punk rock girl. There is nothing in this world you can't conquer."

She tilts her small head, softening her features and giving me a smile that makes hard days worth it. Cerberus walks into the room laying at the bottom of the tub because he hates leaving Charlotte alone.

Love didn't heal my past. It didn't take Charlotte's fear away.

Love is being scared but doing it away because it makes life worth it.

"And when I can't be brave?" She whispers.

"I'll be brave for you." I reply without hesitation.

Whatever she needs, I'll be that. I'll be whatever she needs. Even if she's afraid.

Even if she forgets me, if her fear comes true and she loses all her memories. I will take the scrapbook that she has started and remind her. I will show her the sticky notes, the pictures, all of it.

I'm worried for her because I know her memories are her greatest treasure, but I'm not worried for me.

Because even if that happens, even if one day she forgets everything...

I'll still remember. I'll remember where all her tattoos are. I'll remember the time I came home to the kitchen almost on fire because she was cooking dinner. I will remember the first time I kissed her and the first time we touched.

I'll remember so that she doesn't have to.

Because love, this love, our love?

It's hurting for them, so they can heal.

The End.

Make sure you add book four of the Chicago Fury Series to your TBR
Don't miss reading about Emerson in his standalone
Suicide Pass, coming early 2021

Acknowledgments

Two years ago I saw two people in Starbucks and they were the seed of Malakai and Charlotte. I mean it when I say that every character I write is inspired by someone I have seen or come in contact with. I was eating one of the lemon cakes, drinking my cold brew, and working on a class assignment when I looked up. The guy was wearing a beanie, one that covered the back of his head and held all his hair but you just knew there were mountains of gorgeous locks underneath it. He was heavily tattooed and he was reading Looking for Alaska by John Green. I nearly fainted because it's my favorite book by him. But it gave me a story, a story about this quiet, tall, intimidating man just wanted his very own Alaska, a mystery of his very own, so I gave him Charlotte, his moon-eyes. The girl, who did have blue hair kept looking up at him from her laptop. She was pretty, in a cool way. I was extremely jealous of her nose, it was a little crooked but perfect for her face. And she had this huge headphone over her ears that made her look even cooler. Everything about her seemed unique and different. And she was awestruck by him. All he would've needed to do was look up from his book for a moment, one second and he would've seen her in front of him, but he never did. She left before he never saw her and it broke my romantic heart. But that's fine. They didn't know a writer was watching them. They may never have met, talked, fallen in love, but in this book, they have a happy ending.

Cut from the cute story, because now I have people to thank.

Fletcher, who is trying to learn the in's and out's of the book world just for me.

The Muses, who still make time to talk me out of rabbit holes and read the first drafts. Thankful for you three every day.

Shauna, the strongest woman I know. Who never stops believing in me, even when I stop believing in myself. You are unstoppable.

Stevie, Amber, Jen, thank you for reading and hyping me up. You have no idea how many times I needed it throughout this writing process. You all rock.

And finally, the readers, thank you for allowing me to tell you my character's stories. They are tired of being stuck in my head. You give them a home.

With all my love,

-MJ

Before You Go

If you or someone you know has been sexually assaulted or is a victim of sexual abuse and they are struggling, please visit The National Sexual Violence Resource Center. There you can find out ways help, donate, or just learn about how to prevent and respond to sexual violence.

https://www.nsvrc.org/

About the Author

Monty Jay likes to describe herself as a punk rock kid, with the soul of a gypsy who has a Red Bull addiction. She writes romance novels about insane artists, feisty females, hockey players, and many more.

When she isn't writing she can be found reading anything Stephen King, getting a tattoo, or eating cold pizza.

Also by Monty Jay .

Love & Hockey

Ice Hearts

Made in the USA
Columbia, SC
11 March 2022

57513063R00114